GW01150486

The Conduit

by
Melissa Barker-Simpson

AuthorHouse™ UK Ltd.
500 Avebury Boulevard
Central Milton Keynes, MK9 2BE
www.authorhouse.co.uk
Phone: 08001974150

© 2008 Melissa Barker-Simpson. All rights reserved.

No part of this book may be reproduced, stored in a retrieval system, or transmitted by any means without the written permission of the author.

First published by AuthorHouse   5/30/2008

ISBN: 978-1-4343-7215-4 (sc)
ISBN: 978-1-4343-7216-1 (hc)

Printed in the United States of America
Bloomington, Indiana

This book is printed on acid-free paper.

CHAPTER ONE

Dear Matt

I wish I had stayed in bed this morning. If my day had been a series of pictures or in written form, I would gladly rub it all out and start again. I know what you're thinking - I'm such a 'Drama Queen,' but as the saying goes, 'I've been having one of those days all week!' No, scratch that and make it all month, or better yet, all year!

Anyway, just checking in; I'm going to lie down with my duvet and pretend today never happened. I'll tell you about it tomorrow when I'm in a better frame of mind!
Until tomorrow,
Goodnight, sweet man,
All my love,
Laura

Laura put down the pen, and leaned back in her chair. A sigh escaped her as she thought of the words that were still clouding her mind; the things she wanted to say but couldn't. She loved sitting at the worn wooden desk that had been her fathers. It was battered around the edges, but it was her favourite piece of furniture; it held many family secrets. Now, it was her turn to sit beside its solid oak frame and gain strength from the memories it contained.

Everyday, she would sit and write her letters, cocooned in the familiarity of it. She could almost hear her younger self laughing as she dashed underneath the desk to hide from her friends. It gave her an odd kind of strength. Laura had been writing to Matt without fail, for a little over a year. The counsellor she was assigned, convinced her it was a good source of therapy; it did make Laura feel a little better. Matt used to perch at the corner of the desk and watch her work sometimes. If she closed her eyes it wasn't hard to picture him laughing down at her.

When she lost her husband eighteen months ago, she lost a big part of herself. Laura's best friends, Jo and Nick, were convinced that by keeping him 'alive' in her diaries, she would never fully recover from her loss. She didn't want to accept that; she clung to her letters like a life line. Laura would never admit it to them, but just for a moment, sat at the old desk, she could pretend he was away somewhere and she didn't feel as lost.

In reality, although she derived great comfort from her journal, it was her friends that helped her through. Nick was her guiding light. Since losing Matt, he had stepped up his friendship duties and now called her at the end of each day, so that she could talk to him about the things that were important to her. Nick would listen, as she relayed the day's events, laughing at the way she added a little drama.

Laura opened the desk draw, which was threatening to spill its contents onto the floor, and replaced the journal. She thought briefly about sorting through the mountain of paperwork on top of the desk, but she didn't really have the energy or the inclination to start such a task. She looked at the magazines she had pushed aside; they were threatening to topple over the edge and perhaps bury her in her own chaos. Laura was amazed by the growing number of publications that she put down to 'read' when she had the time; some were almost a year old and she still hadn't opened the front cover, let alone check out that all important article.

The surrounding area wasn't any better. Her lounge was a clutter of things that she never got time to look at, or had no idea where to file. A number of books were piled in front of the skirting boards, some even doubling as a door stop. The only item in the room without any amount of disarray was the couch. Laura had spent a ridiculous amount of money on the purchase, and most of the time it was worth it. It had the kind of material that moulded to the body like a second skin. She especially liked the way it enveloped her in the folds of its fabric. It wasn't as effective as it once was, mainly because she didn't beat the cushions into submission, they way she had been advised.

Laura looked across at the couch and decided she would spend the next few hours cocooned in amongst the cushions, with her favourite movie and a bottle of wine. She walked over to the closet and began to fight her way through a series of boxes to get to her duvet cover. She was knee deep in her own attempt at organisation when the doorbell sounded, startling her. Cursing under her breath, Laura stumbled back towards her living room and out to her unexpected visitor.

"Hey, Blue!" Nick said, as she pulled back the heavy door. Laura smiled in spite of her mood; he had been calling her that since infant school.

She stood aside to let him in. "It's a good job it's you, I was about to send any unwelcome visitors packing."

"Are you sure I'm safe?" he asked, planting a kiss on her cheek.

"Barely, it's late and I've had a bad day!"

"Well, you can help me eat this, and tell me all about it." Nick held up his offering with a grin.

"Don't you have anything better to do than bug me?" Laura asked over her shoulder, already walking to the kitchen to grab some plates.

"No, my sole purpose in life is to torment you!"

Walking to the wine rack he reached for two glasses and joined her on the couch. This was something of a ritual; it was one of the reasons Laura had managed to keep her head above water for the past twelve months.

"I didn't expect you tonight. I thought you had a hot date?" she said, as they dished Chinese onto two plates in unison.

"I was stood up. There's nothing new on that score - I don't know how they keep resisting the Carey charm!" Nick grinned. He had a smile that lit up his whole face, and it was never far away.

"You're just giving off the wrong signals. Give yourself time, the divorce was harder on you than you admit," Laura said, ruffling his hair.

Nick pulled a face. "We are not going to share our feelings, as you try to drag out my feminine side. If you want to swap girly stories, rent a chick flick, and call Jo!"

"Fine, I don't want to talk about you anyway."

"Of course, you were going to tell me about your day."

Laura sat back against the cushions and regarded him thoughtfully. He always seemed to be there, exactly when she needed a friend; it was uncanny.

"Come on, Blue, I don't have all night, and your food is getting cold."

"Must you insist on calling me that?" she asked, feigning annoyance.

"I couldn't call you anything else; it's retribution for scarring me at a young age."

Laura laughed, remembering the day they met. It was during her blue phase in the first year of Infant school. Everything she owned had been blue; her parents received numerous paintings symbolising the ocean or the sky on a summer's day. Nick would follow her around, generally getting on her nerves as he played one childish prank after the other, until one day, she lost her temper and poured a pot of paint over his head. Not surprisingly at the time, the paint had been blue, and thus she had earned the nickname and a friend for life.

"You were so cute back then," Nick said as though he could see into her head to share the memory.

Laura took a sip of her wine, feeling relaxed for the first time all day. "This is much better than hiding away and swimming in a vat of self pity - it's getting pretty deep. You always seem to appear just when I need you."

"I know, kind of strange that. But then again, I know what you're going to say before you say it. Friendship has obviously formed a bond that is beyond the mortal realm!"

"Oh be quiet, and drink your wine. You'll be telling me next that you're telepathic."

"Not me, though I suppose I could be described as telly-pathetic!" Nick chuckled at his own joke.

"Ha, Ha, don't quit your day job; with lines like that you'd kill an audience in five minutes."

"So, what was so terrible about this day?" Nick asked, ignoring her taunt.

"Where do I start? One of my biggest clients has decided they can provide the service in-house; Jane starts her maternity leave this week; Stephanie just informed me she will be absent for at least another month; and Charlie, my strongest member of staff, just handed in her resignation." Laura stopped to take a breath, before continuing her rant; Nick almost choked on a mouthful of wine. "If that wasn't bad enough, I got hit on by a slime ball at lunch, missed an important meeting because my assignment ran over, and got a flat tyre on my way back to the office. I thought nothing else could happen until I was driving home and hit a suicidal rabbit, who decided to jump in front of the car. I had to watch it gasping for breath, not having the courage to put it out of its misery. I stayed because I couldn't leave it alone."

"I bet you gave it a proper burial," Nick said shaking his head.

"Just a small grave at the side of the road - I kind of felt responsible."

"Well, the rabbit was either suicidal or enjoyed the adrenaline rush from dodging big cars; either way it wasn't your fault. Go back to the beginning and we'll deal with the problems, one step at a time."

Laura took another sip of her wine and buried herself further against the cushions. She took a deep breath and started from the beginning.

The Guardian watched on as Laura talked about her day, taking each problem and gaining new perspective. This time she was animated and relaxed. He sensed that she was feeling giddy, if not from the wine, from the laughter that echoed around the apartment whenever the two friends were together. Laura was in capable hands, so he observed from a distance.

Over the centuries people have referred to his job in many ways; spirit guide and Guardian angel being the two most common. The day Laura was born he had been waiting for her with an anticipation that equalled that of her parents. He enveloped the tiny bundle in love, to keep her safe from harm. Laura had needed this protection at different times in her life; he was always by her side.

The Guardian has the power to become whatever Laura wants or needs him to be. Although he regularly takes on the essence of a man, she has never seen him with an awareness of who he is. Most of the time, she senses that someone is with her and presumes that feeling is her best friend Nick, or at least the spirit of him. Occasionally when he wraps his arms around her, like the bedspread she loves so much, she senses her husband and draws comfort from that.

When Laura needs a little extra support and her Guardian's unseen presence is not enough, he becomes the original shape shifter; a dog she can pet to feel the warmth of a friend; a stranger she has encountered, with a smile to let her know she is not alone; or a bird sitting on her windowsill, instilling her with trust. He does not influence Laura, nor does he have the power to change her decisions. He is more a part of her conscience; offering her strength when she needs it the most.

Chapter Two

From: Nicky
Here's hoping today is not a blanket day! Have a good one Blue. See you tonight…Doc x

Laura pulled into her designated car parking space and prepared herself for a day full of problem solving. She felt more positive, as Nick told her she would, but she was touched by his message all the same.

The building in front of her made her pause for a moment, as it did most days. It was impossible to ignore its bold beauty. Laura had been renting the space for her business almost five years now; she still felt like pinching herself for achieving such a prime location. The stunning architecture was the envy of many; it wasn't surprising that Sowerby Hall dwarfed surrounding buildings, though it didn't look out of place.

Laura's attention went to the gargoyles which sat on top of the great hall; they were the protectors of all who set foot in her. They weren't unsightly or redundant, they didn't look pretentious; they just blended into their surroundings whilst adding character and standing.

Whenever she stood, looking up at the building, her problems seemed less significant. She didn't deny it was a challenge, running a sign language interpreting service, but it wasn't one she faced alone.

Several people passed Laura before she finally entered the building. They were used to this daily ritual. It gave them a chance to chat to one another before they moved on to their respective workplaces.

Laura's attention to detail was meticulous. As she walked along the corridor which led to her section of the building, her eyes took in everything that a visitor could see. It was important to her to create the right environment; one that was friendly and open.

"Good morning, Laura." Rebecca smiled in welcome as she entered the offices.

Laura dropped her briefcase and checked her in-tray. "Hi, Becky, any messages for me?" Rebecca was head of administration, and so efficient she was like an extension of Laura herself.

"Just one from Rosie Abbott," she said, handing Laura a coffee with the message slip.

"Oh, that's great. I'm hoping she will accept a part time contract to cover Jane's hours."

"I'll get her on the phone for you."

"Thanks, hon."

Laura walked through to her office to await the call; it would be the first of many. As manager of the service, she didn't have the luxury of interpreting on a regular basis. There was always too much to do. In some ways she missed interpreting within the community, though she still did what she could. Laura had been a qualified interpreter for ten years, but in reality she had been interpreting in one way or another most of her life. Her parents, and her sister, Samantha, were profoundly deaf; she had been raised in a signing environment and spent much of her time within the deaf community.

She didn't set out to become an interpreter; there were times in fact, growing up, that she hated it. Laura studied a business degree at university, and for many years saw that as her future. She underestimated the power of the language she grew up with. It was a big part of who she was. When she finally decided to further her sign language training she was not surprised at how much she enjoyed interpreting, she was more surprised that she seemed to have a natural talent for the job.

Laura started her career as a freelance interpreter, gaining the experience she needed to establish the service. She now had a team of nine, including three members of staff who made up the administration team.

As she listened to the ringing tone on her intercom, she thought about how far she had come and what an extraordinary team she had. They had stepped in to pick up the slack when Matt died; smoothing things over when she walked around the office like a robot on auto pilot.

"Hello, this is Rosie Abbott, speaking." Laura's attention snapped to the intercom when she heard the husky tones of her colleague filling the room.

She picked up the receiver. "Hi, hon."

"Hey, babe, how are you?"

"Well, how about you?"

"You know me - I never let things get me down. I'm sorry I have to speed this up and cut to the chase, but I keep missing you and now I have a job in ten minutes," Rosie said. There was amusement in her tone.

"I was hoping to beg a favour from you."

"Shoot!"

"I have a slight staffing problem. I'm in the process of advertising a few vacancies, but in the meantime I was wondering if I could subcontract you on a temporary basis, terms to be negotiated?"

"I have some commitments, but we can work around those I'm sure. Why don't I come in to the office and we can talk about practicalities?"

"That's fantastic, thanks, Rosie. I owe you big time."

"How about I come in on Thursday around 9 am?" she continued, the pages of her diary crackling across the phone line.

Laura quickly scanned her own desktop diary. "Sorry, Rosie, I have an appointment."

"Not a problem. My afternoon job should be finished by 6 pm, is that too late?"

"That's terrific. I appreciate you making the effort, I really do."

"Are you kidding? I would love the opportunity to work with you again."

"Ditto, you'll be an asset to the service."

"Well, enough of this mutual appreciation! I will see you soon." The clock was ticking, and she needed to go.

"See you Thursday, honey, and thanks again."

Laura replaced the handset and took a sip of cold coffee. She was thrilled that her first call had gone so well, it gave her the boost she needed to get on with the task at hand.

"I have the job advertisement ready for your approval," Becky said from the doorway.

"You don't need my approval, Becks. Send it as it is." Laura knew that Rebecca would probably insist she checked it, but she liked to play along.

"Jo rang when you were talking to Rosie, she said she has a thirty minute window if you manage to get off the phone in time," Rebecca said, handing the advert to her silently.

Laura continued their charade and scanned the information, before handing it back with a nod. "Thank you, I will call Jo back."

Laura switched the phone to loud speaker and dialled the number. Rebecca laughed as she backed out of the room, when Jo's answering machine kicked in.

"That thirty minutes obviously turned into ten!"

"She's probably ignoring it to make herself look important," Laura said. It wasn't true, and they both knew it.

Jo's family had lived next door to her parents all their lives; they had grown up together and shared many memories. Jo had been immersed in a signing environment from a young age and as she grew, so did her passion for the language. She had known she wanted to become an interpreter long before Laura did; and had a natural affinity for learning languages.

Jo now made up half of a husband and wife team, travelling the country as conference interpreters. Whatever she wanted to talk about, her thirty minute window had obviously been too generous, and Laura would just have to wait. She opened her personal diary and checked when they would be back. Apart from Nick, Jo and Neil were her only social calendar. It had been eight weeks since she last saw them.

That done, she flipped open her note book and checked her list of jobs to do. Laura enjoyed logging her daily tasks because she got to tick them off, and it meant she had achieved something, no matter how small. At the top of the list was a reminder to contact the local primary care trust, who had decided to deal with interpreting provision in-house. Laura wouldn't object if qualified interpreters were being used, but in actual fact the 'in-house' staff were usually sign language beginners who could 'sign' and who would be trying their hand at interpreting, to the detriment of the Deaf community. In this case ignorance was not bliss.

By the time she finished her phone calls, most of the morning was gone. Laura decided to stretch her legs for awhile, and walked into the main office. She was pleased to see that most of the team were in.

"Hiya, Chief!" Phoebe said, beaming up at her. She was sat with her feet up, in the small seating area.

"Hi, everyone. Good morning?" Laura asked.

David saluted her; his usual greeting. "A little heavy, I had a counselling session."

"Did you get an opportunity to debrief with one of the counsellors?" Laura asked.

He rolled his eyes at her, but he was smiling. "Of course, I always do."

"You trained us well, master," Phoebe said.

"Behave yourself, you know what I meant."

"Oh, not fair, you were much easier to wind up yesterday, especially after your melt down!"

Laura laughed. "I just needed a glass of wine and a good moan."

"Poor Nick!" Phoebe said, getting ready to dodge a paperclip or two.

"Watch it, if you're not careful, I'll give you Valerie Stubbs for a month."

"No, please, anything but that."

David laughed and slapped the desk. "I think she deserves it, go on, Laura, it will give the rest of us a break."

Valerie Stubbs was a regular client. No-one on the team liked to interpret for her because she criticised everything they did, almost like a sport.

"How is Nicky?" Charlie asked, purposely changing the subject.

"He's fine. As annoying as ever, I never could get rid of him!"

Phoebe sniggered. "Charlie could find a use for him."

"You're incorrigible!" David said, winking at her. "I don't know how I'd survive a day without you."

"What are you all doing for lunch?" Laura asked. She lived for moments like these; it was rare they were in the office together.

"I've got about an hour," Phoebe said.

"My afternoon job was cancelled, so I'm cool," Charlie added.

David jumped up out of his seat. "Well then, that's perfect, because I have just over an hour. Let's get this show on the road."

"I have some good news to share," Charlie said as they headed for the door. "I may have found someone to replace me." She paused at the door to Rebecca's office. "Are you coming, Becks?"

"I have a lunch date, thanks. You can fill me in later."

"See you in an hour," Laura said, linking Charlie's arm as they turned to follow the others.

They went to their favourite hangout, a place they frequented whenever they managed to grab some free time together. The bar had a European charm, with large comfortable sofas in one room and battered tables in the other. There was a separate restaurant, which had equal appeal. Laura liked the pictures hanging on the walls; a snapshot of every major city around the world. A traditional coffee machine dominated the bar, but the real eye catcher was the chalk boards, enticing even the most distinguished palette with a variety of mouth-watering cuisine. Laura convinced herself it was the atmosphere that kept them coming back for more, but it helped they did a mean latte and banoffee pie.

As she cut into her little slice of heaven, she turned to Charlie. "So, what's all the mystery? Who have you found to replace you?"

"Well, it's kind of exciting because it would bump up the male members of the team. You know how difficult it is to attract male interpreters," Charlie said, winking at David.

Phoebe agreed with her usual flare "Yes, good men are always so hard to find!"

"Be careful, you could cut yourself on that wit!" Laura said. She laughed when Phoebe pulled a face.

"Do you remember Duncan Thomas?" Charlie asked.

Laura felt a pang at the mention of his name. "Of course, he interpreted my wedding!"

"Sorry, I forgot."

"Hey, there's nothing to be sorry for. I haven't heard from Duncan in a while, not since he moved to Australia."

"I remember." Phoebe agreed. "He is an absolute legend in the field of research, nicknamed, the oracle, by most of his students."

"That's right. Rumour has it, he's moving back to Yorkshire and will be looking for work," Charlie said.

Laura looked at her thoughtfully. She was obviously feeling responsible for leaving the team short staffed. "I didn't know that, we sort of lost touch."

"Maybe you could convince him to join the team?" Charlie said hopefully.

"That's a nice thought, hon. But I'm sure he's made plans of his own."

"What a shame. If I remember correctly he's a bit of a dish." Phoebe said.

Laura grinned, knowing Phoebe didn't mean any harm. "You're not his type, sweetie!"

Phoebe smiled wickedly. "It doesn't stop us from having a little eye candy to look at."

"Hey, what am I, chopped meat?" David asked.

"Come on, stud, you don't need us to tell you how gorgeous you are. We'll just have two beautiful people to get us through the day!" Phoebe put her arm around him affectionately.

"You are so shallow!" Charlie said giggling.

"You love it."

"I do, and I'm going to miss you guys so much."

"Speaking of which," Laura said, taking Charlie's hand. "I doubt we will be able to tempt Duncan, no matter how fantastic our team is. But none of that matters, we understand why you can't stay and we don't want you to worry. It won't be the same, but we will be fine."

"Are you kidding? I know that. You are all amazing; any smart person would jump at the chance of joining you."

Laura squeezed her hand reassuringly. It hadn't been Charlie's choice to leave the service. Her husband's promotion came with a price tag; a move to Scotland. It was hard on Charlie; she wanted to support him, but it meant leaving a job she loved. It didn't help that her father was ill and she wouldn't be around to take care of him.

"You could always stay, ditch Gary, and pursue the delightful Mr. Nicholas Cary!" Phoebe said to lighten the mood.

Charlie squeezed her hands together in a throttling motion. "Will you stop already with this obsession about me and Nicky; I have a soft spot for him, but it doesn't mean I'm going to leave my husband!"

"Everyone has a soft spot for Nick. He's one of the most charming men I've ever met," Phoebe said. All eyes turned to her.

"Don't start!"

Everyone laughed, enjoying making Phoebe squirm. It wasn't very often that she backed herself into a corner.

The Guardian watched on as Laura finished lunch with her friends. He was thinking about the possibilities that would undoubtedly present themselves. From time to time he has the power to orchestrate a series of events along Laura's chosen path; she either takes advantage of them or she does not. His role as Guide is more than just watching out for her in a physical sense.

He knows Laura to be a strong individual, who often masks her true feelings from the world. The Guardian also knows how much Laura struggles to let go of her husband; the memories are a healthy stage of the grieving process, but the sorrow she has locked deep inside means her husband is tied to her by an invisible thread.

As Laura left the restaurant to return to work, the Guardian walked in step beside her. This level of contact is not necessary all the time; her spirit reaches out to him when she needs him close by; even if she isn't consciously aware of it. The Guardian has a strong link to Laura; he has only once used that connection to communicate directly with her.

Laura was driving home from work one evening, after a particularly gruelling shift and drifted to sleep at the wheel of her car. He knew she was tired, he had been with her for the entire journey, but his constant attempts to reach her had failed. In desperation he took physical form and touched her shoulder; hoping the shock would rouse her from her sleep. The Guardian also called out her name, the urgency in his tone, coupled with the contact was enough to do the trick.

She often talked about it over the years; questioning what happened. It didn't matter to him what she believed, the important thing was that she did not come to any harm.

"So, how was this day?" Nick asked as they settled down in front of the television.

"I followed your advice and do you know something – it actually worked!"

"Where's the popcorn?" Nick nudged Laura softly. "A movie isn't a movie without popcorn."

"I'll make the popcorn, if you make the coffee."

"Can't we get through a couple of hours without coffee?"

"You know the answer to that!" she said, accepting the hand he held out for her.

"I can't imagine what that stuff is doing to your insides."

"Let me worry about that. Quit bugging me, and help me out here, wise guy."

They worked silently in the kitchen. It was a ritual they carried out many times. Laura handed him the coffee filters as she worked the popcorn machine. The kitchen was small so she didn't have to stretch. Nick seemed to dwarf what little space they had, but she was so used to seeing him there that her movements were almost like part of a dance, as she predicted his next move.

"How come you gave in so easily with my choice of film?" he asked breaking the silence.

She leant against the counter, looking over at him. "I just wanted to say thank you for being there when I need you. I know how busy your schedule is."

"Come on, Blue, it's what I've always done. I love spending time with you. There has to be more to it than that. I can feel a favour coming on!" He handed her a fresh pot of coffee.

"My, we are suspicious. Just because you chose a stinker last week, which is punishable only by several chick flicks, it doesn't mean I can't have a moment of weakness."

"Just ask me and get it over with, I'm not getting any younger."

"Oh, all right. I need you to pick me up from the airport on Tuesday; I checked your schedule and you're not on call."

"You know more about my schedule than I do. When did we become like a married couple?"

"I have to know more about your schedule than you do so I can remind you to have a life outside your work."

"See what I mean!" Nick pulled a face. "Okay, if I'm free I'll do it, though why you can't book a taxi like everyone else."

They walked back into the living room with their snacks. "You can't be serious, and have to speak to another human being at 7.30 in the morning. I wouldn't wish that on anyone but you!"

"What you mean is, that you want someone to analyse with, someone to go through the assignment with, so that you're satisfied you did a good enough job."

"I'm so predictable. What can I say, Nick, you calm my nerves. You know I hate flying so it makes me feel better to know there's someone waiting on the ground," Laura said.

"I'm touched."

"Did I over do it?"

Nick ignored her and pretended to watch the film.

"I should have stopped at 'I'm so predictable'."

When he still said nothing, Laura caved. "All right, all right, you win. But you wouldn't believe me the first time, so I'm not saying it again."

When she saw the smirk on his face, she realised he had known all along. She wanted to strangle him right there and then. "So, you were just playing with me, huh?"

"I have to get my amusement somewhere," Nick said through a mouthful of popcorn.

"Well now it's payback time." Laura reached over and grabbed a handful of popcorn. Before he had a chance to react, she pulled open his sweatshirt and dropped it down his top. Nick recovered quickly; with lightning reflexes his hand curled around hers. He wasn't quite fast enough so she slipped out of his grasp before his grip tightened.

Laura ran behind the sofa, giggling softly. She knew she would pay for the attack. It was agony waiting for Nick to make his move; when it came, it came quickly. Laura only had the chance to shake her head in disbelief as he grabbed her by both wrists and swung her over the top of the sofa in one swift movement. Nick controlled her descent so that she didn't hurt herself when she landed. He pushed her to the back of the sofa, and sat in front of her so that she was pinned to the cushions by his weight. Laura waited a moment until she got her breath back;

she was laughing so hard she felt a little winded. She eventually began to wriggle her way free, but it was no use, she was stuck.

"All right, you got me. Now that you've had your fun, let me go." Laura hoped he was in a generous mood.

Nick ignored her; he was concentrating on the television screen, as though lost in the story. Laura knew it was pretence because he had seen the film a hundred times and could quote every line by heart.

She tried to reason with him. "Come on, Nicky, I said I was sorry."

To frustrate her even further, Nick lifted his sweatshirt and looked casually at the popcorn, stood in a line across his belt like a row of small soldiers. He didn't do anything to brush the sweets away; he took a piece and popped it into his mouth with a smile

"All right, enough already, how many times do you want me to say I'm sorry?"

Nick laughed at the petulant expression on Laura's face, finally moving forward so that she could escape.

Laura stole a piece of popcorn from his belt and put it into her mouth. She retreated to the other side of the couch and stared at him defiantly. "You're getting soft in your old age. I'm surprised you gave in so easily."

"I didn't want you to pout for the rest of the evening and spoil the film. I don't know how long it will be before you go all soft on me again."

Laura thought about hitting him with a cushion and then thought better of it. Their games often got out of hand, and he didn't play fair.

"So shoot me for loving my friend, and wanting to show it," she said instead.

"Don't start that again. I want you to promise you'll be completely quiet, which means no talking through the best parts of the movie."

Laura smiled at him; he didn't realise it, but he mumbled the words under his breath. Nick was usually so engrossed in the film that he wouldn't have heard a word she said. Not that it mattered because Laura loved the movie too; it was one of her favourites. She would never admit that to him of course; that would be no fun at all.

Chapter Three

Dear Laura

I don't know if you will ever get these letters, but I just wanted you to know that I have cherished ever word you have written, and the time you spend sharing your life with me. I miss you, I miss everything about you; your humour, your compassion, your generosity, and most of all your warmth. Thank you for taking care of Sophie, it was sweet of you to go to her first production and I know it meant the world to her.
Until the next time my love,
Forever in your heart,
Matt

James stared at the letter he had written with a mixture of horror and fascination. He often joked that the pen took on a life of its own, channelling something from deep within, but he had almost no memory of writing the words before him. This was the third time it had happened and he couldn't ignore it any longer. Each time he sat down to write his article, a letter fell onto the page, each one addressed to Laura. James had the feeling he was being used as a vessel. It was a strange notion but he couldn't get it out of his head. He still had the other letters; he never discarded anything he wrote. What he needed was another opinion. He had a lunch date with his sister in two days and she would know exactly what to do.

James spun his chair to face the adjacent work surface and turned on his PC, opting to restart his article electronically. He normally wrote the first draft by hand but that obviously wasn't working for him. Waiting for his archaic machine to boot into action usually drove him to distraction so he sorted through his mail again.

At the bottom of the pile, were the shots from his latest assignment. He spread the photographs across his desk, scanning them with a grim expression; it was going to take a miracle to choose a good shot from the entire bunch. He flicked his gaze over them, hoping to find something appealing to the eye. His attention came to rest on the dark haired beauty who facilitated the interview. Her name was Laura Kane. The fact that the letters were addressed to a girl of the same name had not escaped his attention; it could have been a coincidence, but he didn't think so. James couldn't deny that her energy had drawn him in, and he knew that she felt it too. He wanted to pursue the attraction, but unfortunately her barriers were stronger than a fortified castle.

He looked at her photograph closely; she had been caught unaware and obviously felt relaxed at the time of shooting. He remembered the smile, the way it lit the room and for a moment he felt a pang of regret that he hadn't tried harder.

He didn't dwell on that too long, or the fact that he couldn't decide on a shot; his attention soon drifted to the computer screen. James cursed when he saw that he had thirty- two messages in his inbox. With a trained eye, he picked out the ones that needed his immediate attention. He opened one from a colleague first, chuckling at the words in the subject line.

To: james.pearson@momentintime.org.uk
From: barry.fielding@momentintime.org.uk
Subject: Your ass is mine!
Hey, J

You owe me big time, my friend. I expect to see you Friday with your hand in your pocket; it's your round!

When are you going to grace us with your presence?
Later,
Baz

James pressed the reply button, grinning at his own immaturity.

To: barry.fielding@momentintime.org.uk

From: james.pearson@momentintime.org.uk

Subject: Tea for two!

Hi, Barry

Don't pretend you didn't enjoy spending the afternoon sipping tea and swapping knitting patterns. I'm sure you were a complete hit, the only members of the female race who would put up with you for more than an hour!

I do owe you though. See you tomorrow – I'll buy you an espresso!

Yours in debt,

J

James replied to his other e-mails before starting work on the article. His editor was incredibly patient when she felt the piece was worth waiting for. He wasn't under any illusions that this was favouritism, her patience was wearing thin; she would expect the article on her desk by morning.

My moment in time this week took me by surprise and gave my cynical heart a little boost; enough dare I say, that one moment in the lives of my subjects was not quite enough…

James lost himself, as he always did, in his writing. This time when he looked back at his work, he gave a satisfied smile. It was coming together - he was back on target.

He enjoyed the freedom of being a freelance writer. The work could be tough, but he thrived on the challenge. James had a contract with two magazines, so that he could at least guarantee some of his income. He wrote a regular feature for a local magazine, created to raise money for charity. The magazine had started its life as a monthly publication, but due to popular demand, was now circulated weekly.

It usually meant a commitment of two days per week; the work was generally a history piece, aptly named 'Moment In Time'. James identified local projects and explored the developments, better or worse, over the years. There were two other members of the team who worked in a similar way; Barry was the lively one of the bunch, Tony the serious one, with James falling somewhere in between.

James was, for the most part, a loner. He had been most of his life. When he met Tony and Barry, it was almost like gaining a second childhood; he was far less serious. They made him realise what he had missed all those years at university. In those days he had preferred to stay in his room and study; pretty much keeping to himself.

Thinking now about their regular tryst on Friday night, James wondered what Barry was planning. It wasn't difficult to read between the lines of his e-mail, in fact, he was probably in for a dangerous night.

James forced his attention back to the article. He was happy with the first draft, so he attached it to an email and sent it to his brother to proof-read. He had been giving Dennis his work to read since high school and old habits die hard. The arrangement was a silent agreement, and not exactly the norm, but there was no-one he trusted more to do the job; it helped that Dennis majored in English Language.

He knew he was lucky to have such a supportive family; they put up with his insecurities, listened as he read aloud and shouted about how talented he was to anyone who would listen. Just thinking about them made him think about Danielle, his twin, and on impulse he reached for the office phone and dialled her number.

"Hey, Bro." Danielle answered on the third ring; she had caller id, but most of the time she knew it was him without looking.

"Hi, Dan, how are you?"

"Well, thanks. I'm looking forward to our lunch date."

"I have something I need to talk to you about," James said. He desperately needed her advice.

"Sounds mysterious, you're not running off to the other side of the world again are you?"

"No, but knowing you it will give you a bit of a kick!"

"Now I'm really interested. I need something to occupy my days whilst I'm waiting for the baby to come." James caught the melodramatic sigh that travelled down the phone line.

"You make it sound like you're waiting for a delivery from the stork!"

"I wish it was that simple. At least then I wouldn't have to endure child birth," Danielle said.

"Are the nightmares still bothering you?"

"Not as much. George thinks I'm amusing. I had a dream recently that I gave birth to a nine year old; I was devastated that I'd missed out on the early years!"

"Bless you, sweetheart," James said trying hard not to laugh, she was such a sensitive soul.

"What can I say? My hormones are all over the place."

"It won't… hang on a mo, Dan." James' mobile sprang into life beside him. He glanced at the screen; his editor was calling and she didn't like to wait. "I have to go sis, but I'm looking forward to Friday; we'll save it until then," James said hurriedly.

"Can't wait, see you then."

"Bye."

James replaced the receiver, and pressed to accept the incoming call at virtually the same time. He was too late; when he put the phone to his ear, the line was dead.

James tapped on the glass of his editor's door and entered when he heard the usual welcome.

"You wanted to see me?" he said to Grace, smiling as she looked up from a mountain of paperwork. She was the messiest person he knew, but it was organised chaos. She had a sharp mind and knew everything that was happening within the magazine.

"I just wanted to say that you surpassed yourself; the article is by far the best thing you've written," Grace said, direct and to the point as usual; she believed in giving credit where it was due.

"Thanks, I surprised myself too!"

"I have your next assignment." Grace waved her hand to indicate he should take a seat; the only clear space in the room.

"I'm listening."

The phone on Grace's desk buzzed before she got a chance to speak; she plucked it out from underneath the rubble, like a magician pulling a rabbit from a hat. As she listened to the caller, she held her palm in the air to indicate that she needed five minutes. James rose to his feet and motioned to his desk; he preferred to wait there until she finished the call.

"Don't look like that, buddy, you'll do better next time!" Barry said, as he passed James at Grace's door.

"There's only one person who has those conversations, and it's not me!" This was their usual greeting, or certainly insults along those lines. Barry recently bought James a book entitled '101 insults to liven up your dinner party' and they tried to out do one another on a regular basis. It didn't help that their desks were adjacent; at school they would have been split up and probably placed in different classrooms.

"So, did you win any hearts from your last assignment?" James asked. He grinned when Barry showed him the finger.

He had originally been assigned the story. His job was to interview staff and residents at the Hundred Acres Day Service to discover the secret of their recent success. It was an interesting story. The centre had once been used as an institution for people who were mentally ill. Of course, back then, the terminology had not even hinted at equality and people were locked away because they were an embarrassment to society. James would have hated the job thirty years ago; then again he would have derived a certain pleasure exposing some of the monsters who were supposed to be providing the care.

Hundred Acres was now used as a day service for the older members of the community. The staff had many projects aimed at improving the quality of people's lives; the one being reported on for 'Moment In Time' was an innovative scheme working with people suffering from dementia. James asked Barry to exchange assignments for personal reasons, his friend and colleague had accepted without question. James's mother worked at Hundred Acres, so for that reason, he passed the buck.

"I picked up a few numbers!" Barry said to him, fanning himself with a pad of note paper. "What about you stud?"

"I met a beauty, who turned out to be an ice queen!" James replied.

"She blew you out of the water?"

"Big time. I must try harder next time."

Barry rolled his eyes. "You're being summoned," he said, as Grace caught his attention.

"At least somebody wants me!"

James pretended not to hear Barry's parting jibe. He walked back over to Grace's office to find out what she had in store for him next.

The restaurant was usually buzzing with activity, but today, Echo's was all but deserted. It was James's favourite hangout; he met Danielle regularly. It had been something of a custom since college. Not a typical student haunt, Echo's was usually brimming with members of the academic world nonetheless.

As Danielle hadn't arrived yet, James ordered their usual and took a window seat so he could see her arrive. Glancing around him, James's attention was divided between looking for his sister and doing what he loved; people watching.

There were only a few customers, so he had to be careful his watchful glance was not obtrusive. He could not help but study people. James did not judge, or try to eavesdrop on conversation; he merely enjoyed observing the many characteristics of the human spirit. The little nuances that many people miss were James's speciality. Sometimes he would imagine what a persons life was like, playing it out in his head, like characters from his stories. He believed that these observations were part of what shaped his writing, gave it more depth. He questioned his motives today however, and that unsettled him; the letters had really got under his skin.

Just as he was thinking of her, Danielle appeared in his view line. He watched her through the window as she walked towards him. She was immaculate as always; even the stomach protruding in front of her, did nothing to disguise her elegance. They looked alike - not identical twins, but nonetheless they had the same colouring and demeanour. Her long golden brown hair was tied back into a neat bun, and she wore little make-up to hide the large hazel eyes that were a reflection of his.

Danielle smiled when she saw him, rubbing her stomach and raising her eyebrows. James grinned back, rising so that he could greet her at the door. "Hi, Hon, you look wonderful." He hugged her carefully.

"Thanks, today is a good day. Did you order?"

"Yes, I secured us a table. Not that we need it today, I think the regulars have been abducted!"

When they were seated, Danielle observed her brother with interest. "You look tense, you're working too hard."

"It's a combination of things. My work is not really the problem at the moment," James said, retrieving the three letters from his jacket pocket and sliding them across the table.

"I couldn't wait to show you these. I will admit they have me a little freaked out." James hadn't meant to show them so soon, but seeing his sister always allowed him to be honest with himself.

"Who's Laura?" Danielle asked, scanning the first letter.

"Here's the deal. I wrote those letters over the space of a few days, and each time I was supposed to be working on an article."

"I don't understand," Danielle interrupted, preoccupied with the second letter. "Who is Matt?"

"I'm trying to tell you. I started writing and lost myself, which you probably don't think is all that unusual, but the next thing I knew, I produced one of those letters. What I'm saying, and not doing a very good job, is that I have no idea who they are. I just met someone named Laura, but I struggle to find a connection."

James watched his sisters' face for a reaction. Danielle was silent for a long time, looking from her brother to the letters and back to her brother again. "I'm not sure what to say. I can't really think of a logical explanation."

James sighed, looking a little disappointed. "I've given it a great deal of thought. I haven't written fiction for a while, so wondered if the letters were unconscious ideas that were fighting to get onto paper. I know that isn't the answer, but I'm afraid of the true source."

"When was the last one written?"

"Two days ago. I've attempted to write since, and managed to put pen to paper without any more on the mystery couple."

"I need to give this some thought. It may not necessarily be what you're afraid of, and if it is, we need to talk about it instead of avoiding the subject like we usually do. Can I keep the letters for awhile?" Danielle asked.

"Yes, that's fine."

In truth James was relieved that she had offered to help. Once she had recovered from her initial shock, she would be more constructive.

"I'll get back to you as soon as I get my head around it."

"Thanks, I appreciate that. Now, tell me about the nursery, how are the plans coming along?"

Danielle chatted excitedly about the developments; she loved the process of nesting. James was thrilled about having a niece or nephew, he had been involved every step of the pregnancy. Until recently, Danielle was convinced she was carrying twins; her stomach was certainly big enough to house two. Numerous scans, however, had proved that there was only one little miracle. James had been privileged to see the tiny image, when his brother-in-law, Gary, had been called to work in an emergency.

James couldn't help wondering, as he listed to her talk, whether she would romanticise the letters when she talked to Gary about them. Although James was like his sister is many ways, their opinions on the laws of the universe differed considerably. Danielle was a spiritual soul, full of wonder. James was more pragmatic, he knew there had to be a reasonable explanation for the letters, but that didn't mean he could shake the feeling that he wasn't going to like the answer.

Chapter Four

Hi Matt

I finally managed to catch up with Jo today. It turns out she had something of an interpreting dilemma, and you will know from experience, there are usually plenty of those! She's pretty down about it. I think a trip to the cinema is in order. I will ask Nick, the three of us haven't been together in a while.

On a positive note, Sophie is coming to stay with me in a few weeks time. She is really excited, so I'm trying to think of interesting things for her to do. She misses you so much; we all do. I think spending time with me helps her to feel closer to you, if you know what I mean.

Anyway, my love, it is late as usual. I'm going to call it a night – I have a big job tomorrow.

Until next time,

With all my heart,

Laura

Laura reread her journal entry and thought about the past few hours with Jo; she was worried about her. She knew how bad she was feeling because she knew Jo almost as well as she knew herself.

When she dropped her off at home, earlier in the evening, Jo forgot to wave goodbye to her; she rarely did that. It was one of their rituals. When they were small and lived next door to each other, Jo would wait at her door until Laura stepped into her own house. They had done that ever since. If Laura visited for the evening, Jo would normally walk her to her car and stand at the roadside until she had gone.

She decided it was time to call in the cavalry. Nick would jump at the chance to spend time with Jo; he missed her too. In college they regularly went to the movies together; they all enjoyed the long debates afterwards.

Laura walked towards the bedroom, reaching the door just as her mobile rang loudly from the opposite direction; demanding her attention. She looked at the wall clock. It was almost midnight. She hurried towards the annoying sound of her latest ringtone, guessing correctly that her caller was Jo.

"Hi, Hon. I was just thinking about you," Laura said into the handset.

"I wanted to apologise for being such a kill joy earlier. I'm feeling so shitty at the moment and I didn't mean to take it out on you."

"I have a remedy for those winter blues – you, me, and Nicky, the three musketeers - what do you say we get together?"

"I'd love that. I'll phone him tomorrow and we can sort something out between us."

"Sounds perfect. I've missed you; it feels like months since I last saw you. Which reminds me, I forgot to ask how long you're home this time."

"A while, I think. Neil is a little tired of 'the road' as he likes to call it."

"He'd make a good rock star and you a rock chick!"

"I'll leave you with that image," Jo said.

Laura laughed. "Night, rock chick, I'll call you tomorrow."

"Ciao."

Laura sipped her homemade cappuccino as she relaxed on the balcony, grateful for the glorious weather. She let the sunshine wash over her, melting her cares away. She loved lazy Sunday mornings. This was her time, when she could put other things on hold and feel no guilt for taking the time to re-charge her batteries.

Laura closed her eyes, dozing a little. Her body was completely relaxed. So much so that when the telephone rudely interrupted her late morning snooze, her hand jerked in surprise, causing her to spill coffee down her top. She chose to ignore the phone, and instead brushed ineffectually at the stain now spreading across her white shirt. Laura cursed under her breath, she wasn't ready to go back inside yet, but she didn't have a choice now. She was walking across her living room when the answering machine cut in.

"Hi, this is Laura; or rather it is Laura's machine. So if you will leave your name and number, this thing will record the message and I'll be able to get back to you. Thanks, bye!"

Laura stopped at the entrance to her bedroom when she heard Nick's laughter. "You crack me up, you really do. They don't get any better, Blue. I think we need a professional on the job!" Nick was talking about her message - he loved to tease her about them. "Anyway," he continued. "I should get to the point before the machine cuts me off, though I'm sure that would please..." Laura snatched up the receiver before he had time to finish the sentence.

"Hey, Nicky," she said into the handset.

"I thought you'd be there somewhere. I'm sorry to disturb your lazy Sunday morning."

"That's all right."

"I had a rough day yesterday, and I feel like a little of your company. I thought maybe we could go for a picnic this afternoon," Nick said.

"We could each bring a book, and that way you can continue your day of rest and relaxation, being at one with nature!"

"You drive a hard bargain. If you bring the picnic, I'm in," Laura said.

"Done."

"Then I guess I'll see you this afternoon; usual place?"

"Yes," Nick agreed. "The usual place, around 2 p.m."

"Great." Laura suddenly remembered Jo. "By the way, did you hear from Jo yet?"

"Yes, I've given her my schedule for next week so we can sort something out. I asked her if she wanted to meet today but she has something planned with Neil's family."

"That's a shame; she's in need of a little TLC too."

Nick laughed. "I can tell. We'd be a sorry pair if we got together today!"

"I'll have to think of a way to cheer you up - I've got a couple of hours so I'm sure I can come up with something. See you soon."

"See you soon."

As Laura replaced the receiver she thought about the meeting place they had claimed at a young age. There was a nature reserve at the back of her parent's property. As a child Laura would look out of her bedroom window for hours, marvelling at the view. When she was old enough she went exploring. There was an endless array of fields, which eventually led to a river. Crossing a section of this water was an enormous bridge that was both frightening and exhilarating to climb.

On one of her many adventures with Jo and Nick, they found a series of fields that they could run in, and one in particular, with a large oak in the centre, had been their favourite escape. They would sit under the tree for hours, telling one another their secrets. They had even studied under its branches; sheltered from the world. Laura loved it there. When she sat against the trunk and looked around her, all she saw was the beauty of nature and it brought her peace.

Just thinking about it filled Laura with an impatience to be back; she was glad Nick suggested the little trip. She began to plan the arrangements in her head as she went to change. The practical thing to do was to leave her car at her parent's house, which would mean arriving a little early; she would need to pop her head in. The outfit was easy to decide; cool and comfortable. The book, however, was more difficult. Laura only kept a few volumes; the majority of her books were interpreting related. She had a set of *Dickens* that her mum and dad gave her when she graduated university, but she hadn't read them for years.

Laura finally decided on the paperback she started a few months before. She threw it into her bag, along with *David Copperfield* to amuse Nick. She rarely read fiction unless she had to, and if she did happen to be reading something, it was usually light hearted because she didn't have the staying power. Whenever she was on holiday and felt like a soak in the sun, she would buy a romance novel. Something she could relax into and not have to think about too deeply.

When they were in college and had been taking a break from studying, Nick often read aloud to her. He said it was for her own good - he was making sure she had access to the literary greats. Laura agreed because she liked listening to him read and he had a way of bringing a story to life. It was anyone's guess what kind of book he would bring to the picnic.

Laura gathered everything together and hurried to the car. As she did so she began to tap a message to her mother. The thought occurred to her that her parent's might not be at home.

```
To: Mum
```
```
Hi mum. Are you are home? I need to use your house as a car park. I'm meeting Nick! Love daughter number 2! x
```

Laura kept her message short and to the point. English was her mother's second language, so she sometimes found it difficult to access in written form. By the time her mother replied, Laura was sat outside the house, so evidence that they were not at home was un-necessary. The response made her laugh, despite the fact that she now had some time to kill.

```
From: Mum
```
Nicky beat you to it! I am visiting your Aunt Mable. She is unwell and in need of some TLC. I dragged your dad along. Maybe see you later. Love your number one mum x

Laura was over an hour early for the picnic so she decided to make her way to their meeting place ahead of schedule, by travelling the scenic route. It was a beautiful day, and as she walked Laura drank in the breathtaking scenery. There had been days in the past when she had been blind to such beauty, but now she could appreciate the wonders of nature at its finest. She couldn't help but smile to herself when she saw the bridge up ahead; protruding like an iron monster from the depths of the earth. It still looked intimidating, which was no mean fete when you were an adult without the naivety of youth, and the imagination to go with it. Laura was filled with the same exhilaration she had experienced as a child; it made her feel carefree.

As she approached the steps which would take her to the top, Laura felt almost giddy. She raced up them, taking care not to miss a step. There were metal pipes running down the centre of the walkway and though she felt a little foolish, Laura couldn't stop herself from climbing onto them.

She stood for a moment looking around her in wonder. The view hadn't changed much over the years, but her perception of it had evolved. Laura realised she enjoyed the freedom of walking the steps she had travelled in her youth. She was just about to walk on, when she spotted Nick in the distance. She was surprised that almost an hour had passed since she had left her parents house. It was typical of Nick to be early too. As she watched his silhouette getting closer, she felt oddly reckless. Laura jumped off the pipes and climbed onto a support beam so that she could wave to Nick.

"Ahoy there!" she called, liking the echo it caused. Nick didn't respond or signal that he had heard her, so she tried again; this time she tried waving her arms above her head. She realised too late that it was a foolish move. When her foot slipped from under her, her body struggled to balance the extra weight. Her hands had very little to grip onto, so she flailed wildly; flapping her arms to try and regain the balance. Her giddiness from earlier returned, causing the scenery to spin. Laura made one last desperate attempt to regain her footing, but she fell from the bridge towards the water below.

When she hit the surface, the shock of the impact stole the breath from her body. She swallowed a mouthful of water as she gasped for air. Laura returned to the surface kicking her legs wildly, trying to cough the water from her lungs. Pretty soon her body started to burn, her chest screaming in frustration. It only made Laura fight harder.

She was grateful when a strong pair of arms encircled her and she heard Nick's soothing tones. She wasn't aware he had jumped in; he sounded pretty breathless, probably from the sprint to get to the water. Laura allowed him to lead her to the river bank; she put her head against his chest, taking in a huge lungful of air, now that she had the chance to catch her breath.

When they were out of the water, Nick turned to her angrily. "What on earth were you doing? I am so mad with you right now, I could throttle you!"

"You don't need to bother; my throat feels like you've had a pretty good go already!" Laura said, laying her head against the grass.

"When I saw you fall…I…What were you thinking?"

"I don't know. I just felt young and foolish. When I saw you coming across the field, I climbed up so that you could see me."

Nick shook his head. "I'm sorry," he said. "You scared me."

"I kind of scared me too."

They were silent for a moment; Nick lay down next to her and took her hand in his. "Don't suppose you want to get back up there? It will take us forever to back track."

"Sure, give me a minute. I've just had a life threatening experience!"

Nick laughed. "And for once you're not exaggerating."

"Maybe a little!" she said, pushing a strand of hair from his eyes.

"I suppose I'd better go and retrieve the picnic." Nick made no attempt to move.

"Oh, no! Where did my bag go?" Laura shot into a sitting position, looking towards the water mournfully.

Nick got to his feet and went to the banks edge. He scanned the water before disappearing, and returning a few moments later with a soaking item that had previously been her bag.

"I'm surprised it didn't sink to the bottom," Nick said, handing it over.

"Me too, lucky for me it didn't; my car keys are in there and a limited edition *Dickens* novel."

"You're lucky we're having a good summer; it will dry out pretty quickly - us too for that matter."

For the first time, Laura noticed how wet they were. Nick's jeans were now a dark blue and the t-shirt he was wearing fitted to the contours of his body a little too well. "I'm glad none of your young admirers' are here; you look sexy wet – we'd never get to the picnic."

Nick shook his head. "Stop ogling me and come help with the rescue mission."

"Rescue mission?"

"Our lunch."

"Of course!" Laura said, allowing him to help her to her feet.

They walked back across the field to collect the picnic basket. It was in surprisingly good condition to say that it had been abandoned. Laura felt a little guilty that she caused such a fuss, but it wasn't the first time her friend had come to the rescue and it probably wouldn't be the last.

As they walked to their picnic spot, Laura checked the contents of her bag. She had only brought a few coins in an old purse so her money was still in tact, but her mobile had seen better days. She was upset about spoiling the book; its pages would swell and become distorted as they dried. But she knew it could have been worse; she had gained another memory from it at least.

Her thin blouse had already started to dry and her trousers, though a little uncomfortable, would not take long. Luckily, Nick had brought along a pair of shorts, so when they arrived at their destination he quickly changed.

Laura spread out a blanket, which they retrieved with the basket, and placed the contents of her bag in the sun. She then began to unpack the picnic.

"This all looks really good," she said as Nick rejoined her.

"Thanks. I aim to please."

"Seriously though, honey; you've gone to a lot of trouble."

"I just wanted a pleasant day and to take my mind off things. I'm not sure about the pleasant part, but you've certainly kept my mind occupied so far!" Nick teased her.

"So, what happened yesterday? Do you want to talk about it?"

"Not particularly," Nick admitted. "We lost a child and it was hard, but doing things like this, with you, makes it bearable."

Laura knew he took the death of a patient hard, but when it was a child, the blow was particularly cruel. She reached out to him and gave him a hug; squeezing him with affection. "A dose of TLC for the doctor, coming right up."

"I just need to sit here with someone I care about and not be alone right now," Nick said, smiling at her.

"I get it - no talking, no fussing, just sitting. I tell you what; I'll read to you for a change. That way you can relax and not have to say another word until you're ready."

"I'd like that," Nick said.

"There's just one problem."

"What's that - you can't read?"

"Hilarious! My books are a little worse for wear so I need to use yours," Laura said, grinning sheepishly at him.

"It happens to be one of your favourites, actually."

"You brought *Treasure Island*?" Laura asked him.

"I know what you're going to say. But it will be good for me to picture Jamie in an adventure such as the ones between these pages." He handed her the book.

Laura was surprised Nick used his patient's name; he didn't normally. She wondered how old the child had been and how well Nick knew him.

She made herself comfortable; sitting back against the trunk of the tree. "Let's read it for Jamie then," she said.

"Thanks, Blue." Nick sat back too.

Laura opened the well worn pages of *Treasure Island;* it was the only book she could read time and time again without getting tired of the story. As soon as she began, Laura was lost; she realised that she enjoyed reading aloud because it took her in, like no other form of reading.

After a while, Nick stretched himself out and laid his head in her lap; he seemed to be enjoying their adventure, courtesy of *Stevenson.* The next time Laura glanced at him she was not surprised to find he had fallen asleep; judging from the dark circles under his eyes, he hadn't slept last night. She pushed away the strand of hair that always seemed to be dangling near his eyes and continued to read. She knew that if she stopped he would probably wake up, and he needed the rest.

Chapter Five

```
From: Thomas Duncan
```
Just confirming our meeting for 12 pm. I will be the one with the incredible tan and fake Australian accent! See you soon x

The smell of scented apples met Laura as she opened her office door, and for a moment she worried that she had forgotten to throw away her fruit before the weekend. She saw then that Rebecca had placed a few candles on her windowsill. The oversized cushions on the seats and the pictures on her walls, made her office look more like a living room than a work space. The vibrant colour scheme did nothing to tone the informal atmosphere, but Laura believed it created a feeling of warmth and relaxation.

"Too much?" Rebecca asked as she approached.

Laura turned to her, smiling. "Absolutely not; it's a lovely smell." She indicated the coffee. "That one is better though."

Rebecca shook her had in resignation. "People will think you have a serious problem; give it an hour and you won't smell the fruit."

Laura put her hand on Rebecca's arm. "To be honest with you, I'm a little nervous about my meeting with Duncan. Don't get me wrong, I'm curious too, but I'm sure the request has nothing to do with his desire to work with us. I suppose one can live in hope."

"I'm surprised they aren't queuing at the door to work here," Rebecca said.

"That's because you're biased! Yes, we have a good team, but you know as well as I do how long it takes to get the dynamics right; we've had our fair share of complaints."

Rebecca dismissed this with a wave of her hand. "Usually about things that were beyond our control. I see your point though, about the current working environment; we've had bad ones, but they're all good kids." She started to walk back to her office. "I'll let you get things organised."

"Thanks, Becks – you're one in a million."

Laura sat down in front of the computer, and took a grateful sip of coffee. She knew Rebecca was right; she really did need to do something about her addiction to caffeine. Before long, she was lost in her work.

The 'to do' list seemed to have multiplied whilst she was out of the office, so she had plenty to keep her busy.

The service was ticking over nicely, according to her online accounts. It was all thanks to an excellent administration system. That fact that she had time to manage things, now that she had reduced her interpreting hours, certainly helped. Laura understood the importance of being a manager in appearance and not just on paper. She also discovered that being in the office made her feel like a bigger part of the team.

Laura was so engrossed in her task that she was oblivious to the passing of time. When she heard a knock at her office door, she glanced at the clock in surprise; a whole morning had disappeared. "Come in," she called, wondering if Duncan had arrived for their meeting.

"It's only me," Rebecca said, swinging the door open. "The food I ordered has arrived, shall I bring it through now?"

"That would be great, thanks," Laura said following her out.

Rebecca, as efficient as ever, had ordered a large selection of sandwiches and other finger-food, for the meeting. Laura relied on her organisational skills more than she should; it was dangerously easy to become complacent. She sometimes wondered if anything would get done, if they didn't have 'super secretary' to pick up the slack.

"Get those thoughts out of your head, I'm no superwoman. I'm just doing my job," Rebecca said, making her jump.

"So now you have added mind reading to your resume?"

"I just know that look. You can't hide anything from me."

"I know."

They had been working together for five years; Laura had persuaded Rebecca to join her in the early stages of planning the service. The move to setup her business coincided with her father's retirement. The benefits for Laura were two fold; not only did he have the time to offer sound advice, she also inherited his secretary. It was the smartest move she ever made; the foundations were essential in any business, and Rebecca certainly made sure that all the basics were taken care of.

Laura looked across at her, as they worked side by side to set the table in her office; she was still thinking of those early days when Rebecca had taken the lead. "Do you remember…?"

"Hello?" Laura was interrupted by a voice from the other room.

Rebecca instantly rushed to meet their guest. "I'm sorry about that, Duncan; we were just setting things up for the meeting."

He brushed off her apology. "Don't worry; your assistant told me there is a promise of lunch, so organise away."

Laura listened to this exchange with a smile. She gave them a moment before she walked through to give Duncan a hug.

"You look terrific," she said to him.

"You look good too"

"It's been too long; we have a lot of catching up to do. Let's start with that lunch we promised you."

"Sounds great." He turned to Rebecca. "Thanks," he said, before following Laura into her office.

"This all looks delicious. Do you mind if I dig in, I'm starving?"

Laura handed him a plate. "Knock yourself out! You want coffee with that?"

"What, no fries?" he joked, tucking into the spread with relish.

They talked easily whilst they ate. The years seemed to fall away; Laura had always enjoyed his company. Duncan talked about his travels, making her laugh with his stories about interpreting in other countries. When the subject turned to the last time they had seen each other, Duncan grew serious.

"I was sorry to hear about Matt," he said.

"Thanks, I got your card."

Laura told him about the past couple of years, and how she had managed to deal with her grief with support from her friends; especially Nick.

"How is the sexy doctor?" Duncan asked.

Laura laughed at the description. "He's good, thanks."

"I'm glad you managed to get through it. You look really well."

"Life is short, isn't that what they say? I am fortunate in so many ways, and it gets a little easier every day," Laura said.

She got up to make a fresh pot of coffee, her mind turning to the reason she had arranged the meeting. "Now, getting down to business, so to speak. I called you here because I heard you are looking for a temporary stop-gap."

"You heard right. I need something that gives me the time to setup a new course. That is the main reason I came back – I want to teach over here."

"How long do you estimate that will take?" Laura asked.

"Well, in truth, I'm ready to work with a strong team, and your service has endless possibilities for joint working."

"I'm not sure what you mean exactly."

Duncan took a moment to sip his coffee, collecting his thoughts. "It's a little early, but I've been working on a business proposition. I would like to provide all the training for in-house staff, as well as freelance terps in the area. In terms of professional development, I think we have much to offer."

"That sounds interesting," Laura said genuinely. "Are you telling me that until you finalise this proposal you would like to work as part of our team?"

"Yes, that's what I'm saying."

Laura could barely contain her excitement. "That's wonderful news."

"I thought you'd say that. Stuart, on the other hand, told me you would send me packing because you were born with more sense!"

"How is Stu pot?" Laura asked. Stuart Cunningham was Duncan's long time partner; he had been Laura's teacher.

"Only you could get away with calling him that! He sends his love, and to quote him, 'a big sloppy kiss!'"

"I've missed them!" Laura said laughing.

When a person met Stuart they had one of two reactions; they either loved him or they hated him. Laura had taken an instant liking to him. To her, he had simply been an inspirational teacher, and love or hate him, no-one could deny his talent for linguistics or fail to be impressed by his knowledge.

"Make sure you bring him when you come to meet the team."

"I'll do that," Stuart agreed.

They talked about local issues for awhile; Laura gave him information on the service and the team he would be joining. Duncan knew a few of them, and was looking forward to meeting everybody. They worked out a few of the details, and talked more about his proposal. It left Laura with a lot to think about; she had never contemplated taking on a partner, but good training was hard to find, and a person with Duncan's expertise would be an asset to the service.

Laura's bathwater was starting to turn cold; she had been submerged in the heat for half an hour, and still her body felt tense. She was prone to insomnia, and never really found a technique to help her relax when sleep evaded her.

Laura got out of the bath and put on an old tracksuit. She decided to try watching television for awhile, as that sometimes did the trick. It was already 3.30 a.m., so her options were limited on that score. When her mobile phone began to ring, and Laura noticed that it was Nick's work phone from her ID, she knew something was wrong.

She picked up the handset, hoping for some wisecrack that would put her mind at rest. "Hi, Nicky." There was silence at the other end of the phone line. "Nicky, what is it? What's wrong?"

"It's Dad. He was brought in...his heart...he..." Nick tried to get the words out, but he was battling with the panic, making it difficult to speak.

"I'll be right there." She caught Nick's 'Thanks' as she hung up the phone.

On the drive to the hospital, Laura broke all speed limits outside of a built up area. She wasn't thinking rationally so she wasn't in full control of her car, especially as such speed. Laura recognised this, and forced herself to slow down. When she arrived and couldn't find a parking space, she mounted the curb, unconcerned by the risk of getting a ticket. She walked towards the entrance, thinking of Nick; instinctively picking up speed.

She imagined that being a doctor was both the worst and best thing for Nick right now. Laura remembered when they were kids; he was always bandaging up her dolls and other toys, setting up an elaborate clinic and even allowing her to join in. He had a natural affinity for healing people, but whenever someone he cared about was injured he fell apart. When Laura went into hospital three years ago, for a routine appendectomy, Nick had insisted on being present during the operation and had pulled all the necessary strings. In recovery, he had fussed over Laura like a mother hen; even though he had performed the operation himself a hundred times, and knew it was routine.

It seemed to take forever to find him. As Laura walked down corridor after corridor she began to suspect she was in a maze of her own making. She hadn't paid attention to any of the signs; she just wanted to reach Nick. When she rounded a corner and saw him at last, the look on his face stopped her in her tracks; enough to ground her. She practically ran to fill the distance between them, and stood on her tiptoes so that she could wrap her arms around him. She didn't say anything; she didn't need to.

"I don't think I can stand it if he doesn't make it," Nick said, his voice raw with emotion.

"He's as strong as an ox and he will fight this every step of the way."

Nick held her away from him. "Thank you, I'm glad you're here."

"Where else would I be?"

"I know, Blue. I'm just glad."

Laura smiled up at him; he sounded like the little boy who had first given her that nickname.

"What's happening now?" she asked him.

"He's in recovery; mum's in there with him." Nick indicated a room over his shoulder.

"Do you want to sit out here for a while and give her some space, or go in and join them?"

"I just want to be with Dad," Nick said.

Laura didn't say anything else; she took his hand and led the way.

The Guardian was touched by the scene before him. He was not surprised by the depth of love Laura felt for her friend, part of his job was to fortify it. The thing that moved him was the simple fact that they had become so in-tune with one another, they knew instinctively what the other needed.

He had watched them both grow; the closeness they shared was a rarity; one they could not even comprehend. He could feel the pull in Laura's heart – it was going to be a tough time for them. Their personal circumstances were about to change, as was their relationship, but Nick needed her at this moment and no-one could deny him that. He knew that Laura gave her friend comfort when so few others could – those that were visible to him and those that were not. The Guardian could sense Nick's own guide ahead of them, in the room where his father lay sleeping.

His energy was needed in that very room, but in a sense, it was Laura's own special connection to the family that would see them through. As the Guardian walked by Laura's side, he focused his attention on the scene playing out before him. He could sense Laura waver when she saw Nick's father, so he placed a hand on her shoulder and whispered the words that would give her the strength to help her friend.

Chapter Six

To: Joanna@terpterp.org.uk

From: lauraBSL@interpreter.co.uk

Subject: I need your help.

Hi Honey

I left a message on your answering machine, but I just wanted to cover all bases. I need to talk to you, I can't tell you via this medium, but it concerns Mr. C (both of them).

Call me x x

Laura awoke with a start, a little disorientated when she didn't immediately recognise her surroundings. It took a few moments to realise she was still in the hospital and then she remembered Nick had insisted she rest in his office for awhile. Rising slowly she brushed her tongue along her teeth and instantly wished she had a toothbrush; coffee was not a good residue when consumed in large amounts, especially the following morning.

If her car had not been towed away, Laura intended to retrieve her overnight bag as quickly as she could. It was useful being prepared for an overnight stay at short notice; some people were organised by nature, but she had just been caught out too many times.

On the way to the door Laura spotted the photographs that Nick kept on his wall and stopped to admire them. The one with his parents at graduation brought a tear to her eye. She wiped it away quickly, and concentrated on the rest of the collage. Laura remembered painstakingly piecing it together – she smiled as her eyes rested on the terrible trio in college. She loved that picture because it had been an important period in all of their lives. Laura was grateful that they were still as close as they were on that day, and suspected that Jo was the glue that held them together.

She ran her hand across the glass, as she made her way to the door; she was so distracted she almost collided with Nick on her way out of the office. He looked exhausted, but better than he had the previous evening.

"Hey, sleeping beauty," he said ruffling her hair.

"Hi, yourself." She planted a kiss on his cheek. "I was just going to get my overnight bag and freshen up. I feel like something crawled into my mouth and died during the night!"

"Nice!" Nick said pulling a face.

"How's your dad?"

"He had a good night. You were right; he still has a lot of fight left in him."

"I'm always right!" Laura teased. She was relieved to see that the haunted look had left her friend's eyes - they were so expressive that she could tell instantly how he was feeling. Nick had a way of really looking at a person when they spoke, and she loved that about him.

"What about work?" Nick asked.

"I'm my own boss so I can pull a few strings now and then! I need to ring in though, because I'm supposed to be covering a job."

"As much as I appreciate it, I'm fine really."

"I suppose I could come back this afternoon," she said, unsure of what to do. They had been friends for a long time so she knew he would tell her if he needed her to stay, but she couldn't help wanting to do the right thing.

"That would be nice. Now scoot!" Nick told her, pointing towards the door.

"If you're sure?"

"Go. I will be fine, honestly."

"I'll be back as soon as I can," Laura finally agreed, giving him a quick hug and walking through the doorway before she changed her mind.

On her way out of the hospital she looked in on Nick's father. His colour was better, and he looked a little more like the Mr. C she knew and loved; she was glad he was holding his own. As she tiptoed into the room she noticed Nick's mother dozing softly at his side; her hand still holding his. She didn't want to disturb either of them, so she backed out again quietly and went straight to her car. Laura didn't have time to go home, so she called ahead to Rebecca, and asked her to put on a strong pot of coffee; she would have to freshen up at the office.

Laura practically dragged herself into the office later that afternoon, she couldn't remember the last time she felt so tired.

"It looks like you're in need of an industrial sized coffee!" Becky said as she passed her office. "How did the job go?"

"Hard work - David is just behind me. He was an excellent co-worker; he practically carried me!"

"That isn't true, but thanks anyway," David said making her jump, she hadn't heard his approach.

"It is true. It was a tough meeting and you did an excellent job."

"Thanks chief!"

"Phoebe is a bad influence - I don't need you winding me up too!"

"Who's the grump that didn't get enough sleep?" David teased.

"That would be me, so you had better be careful mister!"

"Now, now, children, play nicely," Becky joined in, handing them each a coffee.

Laura walked into the main office, and shrugged herself out of her jacket. She sat down in the nearest seat; hugging her coffee like a prized possession. David joined her, stretching his long legs out in front of him.

"I can't believe we've been working together all morning and you still haven't told me – how did you manage to persuade Duncan Thomas to join the team?" he asked.

"I didn't have to do any persuading. He wants to work as part of a team for awhile, so that he can concentrate on teaching and writing course criteria." Laura gave him a summary of their conversation.

"That's cool!"

"I couldn't agree more, but I can go one better - Rosie Abbott agreed to join us for three months. She starts in two weeks."

"Then the fun will really start."

Laura nodded in response; she was glad her team were supportive of her managerial decisions. They would soon be back to their usual capacity so she could breathe easy again; safe in the knowledge that she had a skilled workforce.

"Do you know, that assignment took more out of me than I realised – my head is pounding," David said, closing his eyes for a moment.

"I meant what I said - you did good."

"I know, thanks for your support. It was particularly challenging, voicing the information about Billy's abuse; I just hope I gave an accurate account."

"You reflected him very well. It was a good translation, and you didn't miss any of the nuances that can be overlooked in high pressure situations. It was the right level of equivalence and you should be proud of yourself," Laura told him, meaning every word.

He was particularly skilled at reflecting the speaker in his translations from BSL to English and vice versa. David had been a straight A student in college and achieved a first in his degree. He had picked up sign language very quickly and achieved his qualification in half the time it normally takes. Laura felt confident enough to send him to any assignment.

No matter how long she had been interpreting there were always new situations, and some areas that still made her anxious. Laura believed she was a good interpreter, but she had her limitations and she knew exactly which jobs to assign to each member of her staff when the chips were down. David was versatile; he wasn't good at everything, but as near as damn it; it would be a sorry day when the service lost him.

"What are you thinking about?" he asked her.

"She's thinking about coming on a long lunch with me!" Jo said from the doorway and they both turned to face her.

"Wow, we have royalty, Laura; roll out the red carpet!" David said, rising to give her a hug.

"Phoebe just made a similar quip in the car park. I don't know which one of you influences the other, though I have my suspicions," Jo replied, smiling past him to Laura.

"Sorry about all the messages," Laura said, moving her feet from the seat opposite so she could sit down. "How's Nick?"

"I didn't get a chance to see him. Mr. C is doing a little better, but I'm sure you know all that."

"I saw him this morning before I came to work. We can catch up over lunch. I'm glad you came."

Jo nodded, turning to David so he didn't feel left out. "How many seconds do you think before I have a cup of coffee in this hand?" she said winking at them both and counting the seconds on her hand.

"I heard that, and I'm busy," Becky shouted from her office. Jo laughed wickedly, continuing to count on her hand.

"I also have x-ray vision, so you can stop counting in sign language!" They all laughed then, sharing the joke.

"I'll make a fresh pot if Phoebe is on her way in too," David offered, rising to his feet again.

"Just make one for yourself and Phoebe – I'm going to take my friend for a late lunch. I won't do anything productive after that last job anyway," Laura said, draining the last of her coffee.

"No worries Chief, I know exactly how you feel." David mopped his brow in a dramatic fashion, which made Jo giggle.

"You can go home early too, if you have nothing else booked in," Laura said, knowing that despite his humour, the job had been a taxing one.

"I have a doctor's appointment to do. I'll slope off after that, thanks."

Laura turned to Jo. "Shall we hit the road then, Mrs. H?"

"You haven't called me that in years," Jo said, following her to the door.

"It must be sleep deprivation - I know you don't like it!"

"I do. I just haven't heard it in a while." Jo poked her head through Becky's office door on the way out. "Bye, my lovely!" she said to her, the grin on her face apology enough for her earlier cheekiness.

"Bye, hon; make sure you stop by before you go off again and we don't see you for months," Becky said.

"Will do."

Laura linked her arm through Jo's, half pulling her out of the room. "See you later, Becks. Call me if you need anything," she said, and walked down the ramp which led to the exit.

She turned to her friend. "Where to?"

"A coffee until we decide where to eat. It's better than standing in the street unable to make a decision like we usually do!" Jo replied.

"Good plan."

They walked in silence for a while, not needing to fill the air with small talk. The first café they fell upon was a few streets away from the office. Jo moved into the seating area to grab a table, whilst Laura ordered the coffee. 'The Greasy Spoon' was every bit as greasy as the name suggested, but the service was good, the coffee even better and Jo could be trusted to find the best table in the house.

"You can wipe that look off your face; you're not on the Continent now!" Laura said, pushing a latte over to her side of the table.

They both turned together; surveying their surroundings. The red and white table cloths looked like they belonged in another era and the decorating screamed to be updated. It was like being at a truck stop café, ones you pass on the road but never felt thirsty enough to go inside.

"It has character I'll say that much. I'm really impressed they've added latte to the menu!"

"It's good too, so drink up and we can decide where to eat."

Jo rummaged through her bag for the sweetener. "So, how's Nicky?" she asked.

"Hanging in there. I haven't spoken to him since this morning, I can't reach him."

"I've been having that problem too. I sent him a few text messages so I'm surprised he hasn't phoned me by now."

"He'll call. You know Nicky; he is probably burying his head in the sand."

"I'm glad you were there last night," Jo said, nodding her head in agreement.

"Me too. It was scary; I've never seen him in so much pain. I felt so helpless."

"That's exactly how we felt when you lost Matt. You may not know it, but Nicky was a wreck. He wanted so desperately to make it better," Jo said quietly.

"I did know, and he did make it better; you both did. I would be lost without him, without you too; but he is the one still babysitting me under the pretence that he has nothing better to do."

"I don't think that's why he does it; friends don't need an excuse to spend time with one another. You were always inseparable; he's followed you around since you were five years old!" Jo said, grinning at the expression on Laura's face.

"You make him sound like a faithful dog."

"I don't mean to. You have a strong connection is all that I'm saying, so he is bound to want to spend time with you."

"We all do."

"Of course, and we were a force to be reckoned with in college," Jo agreed.

"We had a ball."

They reminisced for a while, laughing at the pranks they pulled on one another. Jo had been the most inventive, and she somehow managed to stay out of trouble.

"I've decided where we can eat," Jo said after a while. "The new tapas bar near the university; I passed it yesterday. Do you know which one I mean?"

Laura giggled. "Not really, but lead the way." She slid out of the booth, mightily impressed that a decision had been made so soon.

It was a pleasant walk to the restaurant. Jo talked about her decision to spend more time at home. She led an exciting and varied life, travelling to different locations, but she explained to Laura, it was time to put down some roots. Now that Neil was feeling it too, they had both agreed to make the transition.

When they arrived at the tapas bar, Laura glanced at the menu on the display board. It was a little pricey and the food a touch exotic, but she was willing to try anything once. They walked down steps into a large room with low lighting and an intimate atmosphere. It looked a little like a dungeon from the street, but when they were shown to their seat Laura realised it was all part of the charm; they could have been anywhere in the world. As she perused the menu on their table, Laura ordered a bottle of wine. They were served a medium red in glasses so big Jo said they could take a bath in them - it all felt very sophisticated. The music was loud so they struggled to hear, but as interpreters they were used to reading body language and other features that are part of communication.

After almost two hours the restaurant was practically bursting at the seams. They were asked to move to a table where people sat to enjoy a drink following their meal. Laura looked at her watch again, worrying about the time.

"I haven't seen a waiter in about fifteen minutes, should I go on the lookout for our bill and we can be on our way?" Laura asked Jo. She nodded in agreement; rolling her eyes at the company they were sharing the table with. They were being pushed into a corner by a group of men who looked a little worse for wear. They made a few drunken comments about two 'lovely ladies' being out alone, perhaps thinking they were being endearing, when really they were just plain annoying. Laura avoided eye contact, and went in search of a waiter. She finally located someone, though it took some time to explain where they were seated for the meal; Laura wondered how much money they lost during their busiest periods.

When they finally received the bill, they waited another 15 minutes, but no-one came back to retrieve it. Jo picked up the silver tray and walked with Laura in search of someone to give it to.

"This is ridiculous. It almost feels like a windup; maybe someone will jump out with a camera."

Laura laughed. "I can think of a few people who would be tempted."

By now, they had reached the steps which led back to the street, and they still couldn't find anyone to take the money off their hands. The restaurant was a hive of activity; no-one was paying any attention to them.

"We could just walk out of here with this money, and no-one would even know!" Laura said, lowering her voice, even though nobody could hear her over the persistent music. It had been pleasant before; right then it felt like a torture tactic.

"I was just thinking the same thing. What do they expect when you have to call out a search party just to pay a bill!"

"What shall we do?" they both asked at the same time, setting off the giggles.

Laura looked around them. "I don't know, what do you think?"

"Not sure, but I do know I need the toilet!" Jo darted to the door which displayed a neon 'Ladies' sign. Laura followed her in. She was now holding the tray and had to do a juggling act to get into one of the cubicles. As she bent to put the tray on the floor, her mobile fell out of her pocket and missed the toilet by millimetres. She cursed silently and put the mobile on-top of the money. Laura could only imagine how ridiculous she looked.

When Jo saw her playing the contortionist on her way back out, with the tray held high in the air, she burst into laughter. "Anyone would think that tray is made of solid gold, the way you are guarding it. Why is your mobile on there?"

"Don't ask!"

The looks they received on the way out had them in fits of hysterics; Jo, who now had the tray, tripped over several people in an effort to steady herself. When they reached the stairs again, they saw a maître d' coming towards them, so decided the game was up. Jo walked purposely towards him. She couldn't believe it when he turned, halfway down the steps and began to fiddle with some of the wall lights, ignoring the pair completely. Laura and Jo looked at one another, each daring the other to continue up the stairs. In the end, Jo stepped in the maître d's path, just to get his attention.

It wasn't until they reached the top of the stairs that they realised how lucky they were, because guarding the entrance like centurions, were two doormen, who had not been on duty when they arrived. Just realising how close they had come started the laughter again.

As they walked away, Jo leaned into Laura. "I can just see it now. You and me on the run, trying to balance that damn tray as we weave in and out of the crowd."

"What, with that coat?" Laura giggled, looking at Jo's red jacket. "It might as well be an arrow, mapping our direction for pursuit."

"We did the right thing," Jo said breathlessly.

"I know. In all seriousness, we wouldn't have walked away without paying, but for a moment if felt like fun."

"I was waiting for you to tell me to do it, and you were waiting for me. We could never commit a true crime; we would still be at the scene when the police arrived, trying to decide what to do next!" Jo linked her arm through Laura's as they strolled back towards the office.

"That was just so funny; probably one of those moments that is meaningless to anybody else," Laura said. They could get pretty crazy when they let their hair down.

"I had fun too. We don't do this enough."

"I agree. I'm heading over to see Nicky now, do you want to come?"

"Absolutely."

Laura checked her watch. They would be lucky to catch visiting hours. She wasn't unduly concerned because the nursing staff were generally quite accommodating; knowing one of the surgeons didn't hurt either.

The Guardian watched Laura as she sat with her friend's father; alone in the room with only her thoughts and prayers for a man she had known most of her life. It was a powerful image when she took Graham's hand and started to tell him about her day. He moved a little closer to her to make his presence felt, it was an effort to reassure her that they were both in safe hands. Laura smiled, whether in recognition or self conscious awareness, he didn't know for sure.

The Guardian could see that Graham was tired. He was the kind of man who tried to remain strong for the people he cared about; he couldn't tell Laura that he needed to rest because he sensed she needed to be there.

"It's time to go home. Graham is tired. It is important he gets his rest." The Guardian said this gently; his hand still on Laura's shoulder. At the same time, Graham yawned, sealing the deal. Laura realised she was preventing him from sleep due to the incessant talking. Though he protested, Laura decided it was time to leave.

As she walked out of the room, promising to return, the Guardian walked with her.

Chapter Seven

```
From: Sam
Hi sis x We are all meeting at your place - hope that
is o.k.☺ Make some room for us to sit down! Sam x
```

Laura threw her crockery into the dishwasher with a careless disregard for breakages; she had exactly thirty minutes until Jo and Neil arrived and the place was a tip. Samantha watched her in amusement; not even attempting to help her through her crisis.

"I'm glad I can entertain you!" Laura signed as she rushed past her to grab the hoover.

Samantha grinned. "You never do this when I visit."

Samantha's first language was British Sign Language. She was such an expressive communicator that Laura enjoyed interpreting for her, especially as she loved to play with language and had a passion for it.

"Help out your poor sister and grab that duster and polish," Laura said pointing to an array of household cleaners on the work surface.

"I'm above cleaning, it doesn't suit me!"

"Just because you're in front of a television camera six months of the year, it doesn't mean you can't get your hands dirty like the rest of us."

Samantha picked up a tea towel and threw it at Laura in mock disgust. Despite her protests, she set to work on the areas in most need of attention.

Laura returned to the living room. Her sister's boyfriend, Bobby, was relaxing on the sofa, too busy killing computer generated zombies to notice that they were working around him. If she didn't like him so much she would have kicked him off the sofa and banned him until they were finished, but he was good for Sam and their relationship was still quite new.

It was Samantha's idea to invite Jo and Neil, Laura suspected she needed their seal of approval and she counted Jo in any family decision. Nick had already met him, and they hit it off right away. It wasn't unusual, most people liked Nick. She hadn't needed to interpret a great deal either, his receptive skills were improving. Laura was used to interpreting for her family. Matt never learned to sign, he had been happy to get by using gestures. Laura was always amazed at how much he understood with very little knowledge of the language; he had been a natural born communicator.

She shook the thoughts from her head, cursing silently when the doorbell sounded. The lights in her apartment also flashed, to alert her sister; Laura almost knocked over a table lamp when she was plunged momentarily into darkness.

She threw the hoover in her sister's direction and went to answer the door. As soon as she saw Jo, she knew there was something wrong.

"What is it?" Laura asked in sign, to include Samantha and Bobby.

"Have you seen the *Evening Post*?"

"No, should I have?"

"I think you'd better sit down," Jo said.

Laura settled herself among the newly plumped cushions. Jo sat with her; she motioned for Samantha to join them.

"What's all this about?" Laura asked.

Silently, Jo handed her the newspaper; it was folded to the relevant page. Laura scanned the articles. At first, she couldn't see anything but a page full of lonely heart ads, and then she noticed her name.

Dear Laura

I'm sorry to hear about Jo's bad experience at work. I know how much she prides herself on her work ethic. Knowing Jo, I'm sure she did the right thing; or as you interpreters like to call it 'the least harm'.

I have probably thanked you so many times already, unnecessarily I'm sure you are thinking, but I appreciate the time you are spending with Sophie. She is a great kid, and I am a proud big brother; always have been, always will be.

Anyway, I just wanted to let you know that I am always interested in the things you share with me, and that I miss you so very much.

Until the next time my love,
With all my heart,
Matt.

Laura could feel the anger building with every word she read. "Is this someone's idea of a sick joke?" she asked, fighting back the tears.

Jo, who was reading over her shoulder and translating the information for Sam and Bobby, shook her head sadly.

"I honestly don't know. I contacted the newspaper immediately to find out who printed the letter. I was given a contact name."

Laura was still struggling to understand. "I don't get it. Why would someone do this?"

"I think we should contact this person, Mr. Pearson, and find out exactly what's going on," Jo suggested. She put her arm around Laura, and gave her a comforting squeeze.

"I suppose it's too late to phone now?" Laura asked. It was almost 7.30 p.m.

"Well, it's a mobile number, so under the circumstances I think we should find out right now." Jo rummaged in her bag to find the number.

Laura took a deep breath, and tried to get her thoughts in order. She walked over to the phone and took the handset back to the sofa. For a minute she stared at the numbers penned in Jo's neat script. She was a little afraid of the person on the other end.

"You can do this," Samantha said, taking her hand.

Laura smiled weakly. She punched the numbers quickly before she had the chance to change her mind. The ringing was too loud in her ear; it seemed to last an eternity. Finally, an answering machine kicked in;

"Hello, this is James Pearson. I'm sorry I missed your call. If you leave your name and a brief message, I will get back to you as soon as I can. Thank you."

At the beep, Laura squeezed Sam's hand and spoke into the mouthpiece. *"Hello, Mr. Pearson, this is Laura Kane. I want to speak to you about a letter which was printed recently in the Evening Post. I realise it is late, but if you could get back to me tonight, I would appreciate it. My number is 07788 555329, I will be awaiting your call."* Laura pressed the end button, exhaling deeply. She had somehow managed to remain calm and composed, when a storm was building inside of her.

"Do you want us to stay or go?" Jo asked.

"If I'm honest, I feel like being alone for awhile. Why don't the four of you go ahead without me?"

Samantha kissed her on the cheek, stroking her hair briefly. "Let me know when you hear something."

She wasn't aware of them leaving. She vaguely remembered saying goodbye before she shut down completely. Every part of her wanted to believe that Matt had somehow written the letter, but she didn't see how that was possible. The more she thought about it, the worse she felt; she longed to pick up the phone and speak to Nick. She had been wrong about wanting to be alone, she needed a distraction, but Nick had enough problems without her adding to them.

Sitting beside Laura, the Guardian whispered words of reassurance, hoping he could reach her. He hated to see her so confused and upset; his hand in hers was not having any effect.

"Go and get your journal to compare the letters," he said to her.

Laura did not move from her position on the sofa, though she looked around as if searching for something.

"How can someone, other than Matt, reply to something they have not seen? Get the journal, Laura."

When she moved suddenly, he thought he had finally reached her. But instead of retrieving the journal she picked up the newspaper, and looked at the letter again. The Guardian watched as she read the words, her lips moving unconsciously as she did so.

He could hear Matt's voice as she began to speak them softly – he had been with him when Matt paced beside her, answering the thoughts that were in Laura's heart. It was not that Matt read Laura's journals, he didn't need to. Everything she wrote he could hear as if they were spoken aloud.

The Guardian watched Laura closely. As she came to the end of the letter, he saw that she realised they were a direct response to her own; the look of recognition gave him encouragement. As she settled in to await the call, he continued to reassure her that she was not alone.

CHAPTER EIGHT

Dear Laura

I've been thinking about these letters. I think I started to respond in an effort to let you know how much I understand what you're going through. I suppose it's one of the reasons you began a journal, besides the therapeutic benefit. I know that you were not expecting a reply, and it pains me to think that you may misunderstand their purpose. I also realise that your daily ritual is a very personal account of what you are feeling and perhaps not meant to be shared. I did begin by responding as you were writing; I would laugh with you, cry with you and sometimes even finish your sentences. You may wonder what I am rambling about. I am finding it difficult to focus my thoughts. I will end by saying that I began this journey because I wanted you to know that I will always be with you.

Until the next time my love,

Forever in your heart,

Matt

James sat in front of his artificial log fire, staring into the equally artificial flames, without seeing either effect. He was thinking about the latest letter, which he had prepared for publication. The message he picked up on his mobile phone terrified him; so much so that he sat for over an hour with the letter clutched in one hand and the mobile in the other, unsure of how to proceed. James didn't know what he had expected to happen when he printed the letter, but he hadn't really thought that Laura would actually contact him.

He was scared that the whole thing was a trick of the mind, because he had wanted so desperately to get to know her after one meeting. James wondered what his sister would think of this, she had been the one to push him into publishing the letters. He couldn't shake the feeling that the whole situation was going to get worse before the night was through.

He began pacing his living room, trying to build the courage to ring Laura Kane back. With new purpose he went over to the drinks cabinet and poured himself a Jack Daniels. James tried to control the crazy thoughts that were running through his mind, he had been rehearsing what he was going to say; this amused him somewhat because before long he would be standing in front of the mirror, practising the phone call like they did in the movies.

At last, with a little Dutch courage, he punched in the number. It was not difficult to remember, he was good with numbers. The ringing tone in his ear grated along his nerves. James thought it would never stop; he almost wished it wouldn't.

"Hello, Laura Kane speaking."

"Hello, Ms. Kane, my name is James Pearson. I believe you wanted to speak to me about a letter that was printed recently?" James heard her gasp, and knew she had been dreading taking the call as much as he had dreaded making it.

"Yes," Laura said.

For a moment, he didn't know what to say. The silence was excruciating. "I sent the letter to print," he said.

"Has someone put you up to this?" Laura asked. She sounded angry.

"Look, this is a very new and strange situation. I am at a loss to know what to do."

"I don't know what you're talking about. The letter is a fake. There is information in them which leads me to believe they are addressed to me, but they cannot be from my husband because he died almost two years ago."

James didn't know what to say, he had no idea how to explain where the letter came from.

"I… perhaps you could come to the office and we can talk about it. I apologise that this is so upsetting, but I don't think it can be resolved in a phone call," James said.

"Who gave you the letters?" Laura asked, ignoring his suggestion.

"It isn't as simple as that Ms. Kane - no one gave them to me. I really think that you should come by and we can talk things through."

"If no one gave them to you, then how…" she didn't finish the rest of her question. James wondered what was going through her mind. He could hear her ragged breathing as she struggled to come to terms with what he had said.

"All right, can you see me on Monday?" she asked.

"Monday suits me fine," James answered, frantically thinking about where they could meet. If he told her to meet him at Railway House, she would be freaked by the connection to 'Moment In Time'.

"Do I come to the Evening Post?" Laura asked him.

"Yes, that's right. I will sort out a room for us around 9:30 a.m."

"All right, I will see you then." He sensed that Laura was itching to end the call.

He gave her the escape she needed. "See you then."

James sank back into his huge arm chair. He threw the phone onto the side table and felt relief wash over him. He had survived the phone call; now all he had to do was face Laura Kane in person. Without the adrenalin pumping through his body, James felt the usual weariness wash over him. He had worked none stop since he got back from Malaysia eight months ago, and he was in desperate need of a vacation.

Closing his eyes, he felt himself relax; he had arranged to meet Barry in an hour so a little snooze wouldn't hurt.

James opened his eyes and took a few moments to re-orientate himself. It had grown dark outside, and the temperature had dropped considerably. He glanced at the wall clock, cursing when he saw the time. He had slept for three hours, and kept Barry waiting for at least one of them. He stretched to reach the phone, noticing that he had a message.

`From: Barry Fielding`
Hey. Something came up. I will call you later. Sorry I had to bail. Baz

James smiled, amused by the message. Barry was a man of few words. He had probably found a hot date; the reason he had been ditched. Still it let him off the hook. Barry would make his life a living hell if he found out he had slept through their plans. Not that he intended to tell him. Backed into a corner, James would have made up a story to keep the peace; a good one, so at least he was entertaining, if somewhat deceitful.

As he had no immediate plans, he stretched the sleep from his body, and went to make himself something to eat. When he walked into his moderately sized kitchen he couldn't suppress a satisfied smile; this was his domain. If he wasn't so obsessed with literature, he might have been a chef. The workspace was a cook's paradise, with every utensil imaginable laid out in a neat and orderly fashion. Chrome shone everywhere, catching the eye. With all the latest appliances, the kitchen looked like a sci-fi fan's wet dream.

As he methodically began to prepare an omelette, Laura Kane's face came involuntarily into his head; the picture so clear it was almost tangible. When James fell for a woman, he fell hard and fast. The strength of his attraction to Laura had been a powerful aphrodisiac; he wondered for the second time if his own mind had subconsciously created the drama he now found himself in.

James had always had a vivid imagination, so much so, that as he thought of Laura it was almost as though she was there in his kitchen, sharing his light snack. He shook his head with mild amusement as he forked some of the omelette into his mouth. He could really enjoy the fantasy that just popped into his head, but he had to face her soon so he tried to think of something less entertaining. To James's frustration, banishing Laura from his thoughts was not easy; before long he was remembering their first meeting.

A young Deaf artist had caught the attention of many collectors in the field for his innovative yet haunting images. He used hands as a focal point, but the pictures told a story of their own. They quite literally took the breath away; love them or hate them. When James met Donald Stacey he understood instantly the great charisma behind the man, which reflected in his work. He communicated with Donald and his team through a BSL/English interpreter, the lovely, yet distant, Laura Kane. James knew nothing about sign language, but watching her was like witnessing great poetry or seeing someone come alive to music.

When he approached her at lunch, buoyed by the rapport they shared on a professional level, he was surprised at the speed in which she closed in on herself. James made a fool of himself; she probably thought he was a jerk. Laura, on the other hand, was the consummate professional; their disagreement over lunch had not affected the final interview.

James felt embarrassed by the memory. As he washed his plate in the sink, he realised he needed to something to occupy his thoughts or he would continue on a road of mindless torture and over analysis.

He decided on a few hours in the office. It was his sanctuary, a personal retreat from the world. James loved the space; it was more like a library than a place of work. Wall to wall books dominated the room and stole the gaze, as if they were the only feature in it. He traced the spines with his fingertips, searching for an adventure to lose himself in. His volumes were filed according to genre; he had a diverse taste in literature, though he was loyal to his favourites. His fingers stopped on *Dickens;* he pulled out the volume and took it over to his armchair.

His book of choice was *David Copperfield* because it always calmed his nerves and never failed to transport him to another place and time. He settled down in his cosy retreat and allowed the words to wash over him.

CHAPTER NINE

From: nicholas.carey@cfw.co.uk

To: lauraBSL@interpreter.co.uk

Subject: Thanks a million

Hey Blue

I just wanted to say thanks for last night (wink, wink, nudge, nudge!). I know we have this ongoing thing about not showing gratitude, it being 'all part of the service' because we are friends, but I don't know what I would have done without you. I tried to catch you at the hospital earlier, but I was ordered to get some rest and who am I to disobey my mother?

Anyway, I tried to ring you but the answering machine cut in and I didn't want to leave a message; even though I could phone it a hundred times because it always cheers me up to hear your attempts at a message.

My computer is broken at home, so I am tapping away at work. One of these days I will get that system they promised in my office. Luckily I know a few nurses that I keep sweet with chocolate and cookies – they let me use their system whenever possible!

I'll give you a buzz when I can.
Take care
Doc xx

Nick reread the message and pressed send. He hadn't mentioned it in the email, but he had not slept a wink. He was used to long gruelling shifts and was familiar with sleep deprivation, but this was different. Tonight he was not only physically tired, he was emotionally tired too.

His father was no longer in danger, so he had that to be thankful for, but Nick was struggling to come to terms with what happened. He worked in a hospital and saw many patients, but nothing could have prepared him for seeing his father on a stretcher. He had never been sick a day in his life; growing up he seemed like some kind of 'superman' to everyone around him, and Nick realised that he had unrealistically assumed his father was invincible.

As he thought about the past twenty-four hours, he logged off the computer, and went in search of coffee. He took a cup to his mother, who was sitting vigil by his father's bedside. Nick admired his mother's strength. She was putting on a brave face for his father's sake, but Nick knew she had been terrified by the heart attack and still was. As a couple they were very active and travelled all over the world; a generous lifestyle over the past couple of years had not done his father any favours.

"Hi, mum. I brought you caffeine because I couldn't find matchsticks!" Nick said, handing her a black coffee.

"Thanks, Nicholas; I need it. From the look of you, so do you."

"Gee, thanks!"

His mother smiled, stroking his arm briefly before returning to her husband's side.

"Why don't I take over the night shift? Dad will sleep like a baby with all the drugs he has in his system," Nick said; they had been fighting over this for hours.

"I'm fine. This coffee will do the trick. Besides, I don't want him to wake up and find me gone. When he's had another night of restful sleep, I will think about it. I need to go home to get your father some things anyway."

Nick gave in; his mother could be stubborn "All right."

After a brief silence, his mother started to tell him what happened; how scared she had been. They always shared things; it was something he treasured about their relationship.

Nick used to wish he had a brother or sister, until he found something better in his friendship with Laura and Jo. He now had an extended family, and they could talk about their respective parents in confidence, to let off steam now and then. He hardly ever complained about his mother and father; he was an only child and they doted on him. They gave him the freedom he wanted with boundaries that were not too suffocating. Jo's parents, on the other hand, never seemed to be around. They both led busy lives and had no time for the family unit. They eventually divorced when Jo was eighteen and she was devastated by it. She was fortunate to have Laura's parents to turn to, who had adopted her by heart from a very early age. Laura was not without her stresses; living with a dual language and culture was hard on her at times, but now she laughed about the things she would have complained about in her youth.

"What are you thinking about?" his mother asked.

"Jo and Laura, and how supportive they have always been - kind of like sisters."

His mother had a faraway look in her eyes. "They might as well be. Your father refers to them as his daughters anyway. He has a soft spot for Laura, always has; she's a lovely girl."

"I can't disagree with you there!"

"She was here earlier. She asked me to keep a special eye on you and call her if you needed anything."

Nick smiled in response. It wouldn't surprise him if Laura set up camp in the hospital and started organising their lives. "Do you want a fresh coffee? I'm going to grab a few hours on the office couch because I have to work soon. I don't want to make the patients worse than when they arrived."

"Nicholas, you should have told me. I will organise some coffee myself, or the nurses will, they have been looking after me." His mother's face filled with concern. "Are you sure you're up to working?"

"I like to keep busy, you know that. Besides, I can keep an eye on Dad."

"If that's what you need. Now, go get some shut eye, because I know you didn't sleep a wink when I sent you home earlier."

Nick shook his head; he couldn't hide anything from her. He walked to the other side of the bed and kissed her on the cheek. "See you soon, mum. When I come back I will accept no arguments about you going home for a few hours rest.

"Yes, doctor!" she answered, winking at him.

"Good." Nick smiled, walking to the doorway. "Let me know if you need anything."

He checked his father's charts before he left, and made a mental note to chase up test results. Satisfied that everything was in order, Nick headed for his office. He knew he wouldn't have any problem with sleep this time; he was surprised he even made it to the couch.

Nick strolled into the interpreting service, hoping he would find Laura; he hadn't managed to catch up with her in days. He peered through the glass into Becky's office, making a face when she turned to look at him.

"Is the lovely Laura in?" he asked, knowing he was out of luck before Rebecca shook her curls and answered his smile apologetically.

"She has an all day job, I'm afraid. I don't expect her back."

"It was worth a try. I wanted to dust the cobwebs off for a few hours and fancied lunch."

"Charlie's in if you want to say hello. Why don't you whisk her away from her desk - she works too hard," Becky suggested, already pushing the button which would allow him to enter.

"Hey there, Charlie; long time no see," Nick said grinning as he pushed his way into the office.

"Nicky, how lovely to see you." Charlie rose to her feet to give him a quick hug.

"Thanks. How are you?"

"Never mind about me, though I'm well. How are you? More importantly, how is your Dad?"

"Hanging in there; that applies to both of us!" Nick said taking a seat - his large frame dwarfed the office chair.

"Laura has been filling us in. It must have been awful for you."

"It was and is. He isn't out of the woods yet, but I'm an optimist! Why don't I steal you away for lunch and I can bore you with all the details," Nick suggested. Charlie was a nice girl and he needed nice right now.

Charlie reached over to get her bag. "I'd love to."

"Great."

Nick allowed Charlie to pick the restaurant. He didn't get into the city very often, so he was easily guided. Her choice was a simple but elegant café, set back from the main precinct and waiting to be discovered like a small gem.

They fell into easy conversation whilst they waited for their order; it felt good for Nick to discuss his father with someone who didn't have an emotional connection. He made the trip to visit Laura, but wondered if this was a better option because Charlie knew what he was going through. Nick felt an immediate sense of guilt for having those thoughts; he tried to justify them. Laura knew what he felt before he felt it sometimes, and it was nice to speak to someone who didn't go deeper than he was willing to at the moment. He shoved away his feelings of betrayal and concentrated on relaxing for a while in good company; he was just so tired that it was easy to talk without thinking about it.

Lunch was over far too quickly, and Charlie had to go to an appointment. She made him promise to contact her whenever he needed a chat and he appreciated her understanding.

Nick walked for quite some time after she left, not really dwelling on where he was going. The further away from the crowds he got, the happier he became. He almost laughed out loud when he saw two kids playing ahead of him; they looked a lot like brother and sister. The girl must have lagged behind and lost sight of her brother momentarily, because when she rounded the corner he sprung out at her and made her scream in delight at the game. It reminded him of when he was a child, and he had done a similar thing to Laura. He lived on the next street when they were growing up; most of the time she had visited with Jo in tow – but occasionally she visited alone. As Laura prepared to leave at the end of a visit, Nick would say goodbye to her at the door and by the time she had reached the top of the stairs leading away from the house, he had rushed to his hiding spot behind the shed and jumped out on her as she passed by. Laura pretended she hated it, but Nick knew for a fact that she still prepared herself for it when she visited his parent's house.

They had so many memories, the three of them. Nick found it hard to hide anything, and though he managed it occasionally with Laura, never with Jo. He missed her when she was away for long stretches of time, he had neglected her some what on this visit but under the circumstances he knew she would understand. She had visited the hospital earlier, and spent some time with his father. As he walked back in the direction of his car, Nick decided to call her as soon as he got the chance.

Chapter Ten

From: Barry Fielding
You have two hours – tops. I even managed to wangle a coffee and a Danish pastry or two – you owe me big! See you Friday. Barry

James had used up all of his favours to book a room within the *Post*. He was already regretting the agreement to meet Laura there because it was based on a lie he had not corrected; she presumed he worked for the paper. Still, he intended to be completely honest, and he would straighten up that particular misunderstanding before they began their meeting.

He had written another letter yesterday, and it had shaken him because it was an obvious response to someone's personal thoughts; James hadn't decided if he should show it to Laura. He had two others that he had not published and intended to give her at some point during their discussion. James could not explain why he knew that the most recent communications were meant for her eyes; being the third person, and reading such intimate thoughts made him extremely uncomfortable.

James had asked the receptionist to show Laura to the meeting room when she arrived; he was even able to impress her with refreshments on tap. The only problem was his caged animal routine; she was due any moment and from a distance, through glass, he would look like a predatory animal caught in a trap. He forced himself to sit down, only to jump up again when an unfamiliar voice filled the room.

"Mr. Pearson, sir, a Miss Kane has arrived. I will show her through." James chuckled; he was so on edge he was momentarily afraid of an intercom. He didn't want to see her approach, so he busied himself pouring the coffee. When the door opened and Laura was ushered in, he was grateful for the small ice breaker.

"Ah, just in time! Would you care for tea or coffee?" he asked, amusement tugging at the corners of his mouth when he realised she recognised him.

"Coffee would be great; as it comes. I didn't realise when we spoke on the telephone that we'd met; please forgive me, I'm terrible with names." Laura sat down at the conference table; the professional veneer he knew only too well impressed the hell out of him.

"Sugar?" James asked.

"No thanks."

Laura watched him as he laid the refreshments out; he sensed that she wanted to turn around and walk back out of the room. James had a flashback to their telephone conversation. He could feel the tension and he knew he needed to defuse it somehow.

"I realise we have a lot to talk about, but before we begin, I must clear something up." The words tumbled over one another; he was mesmerised by her strong gaze.

When Laura didn't respond, he filled the silence hastily. "Firstly, I apologise for our previous meeting and hope that it won't affect what happens here today. Secondly, I agreed to hold the meeting here because it seemed the easiest option, but I don't actually work for the Post; I'm a freelance writer."

"Thank you for your honesty," Laura said. It sounded like a reprimand and James didn't know how to respond.

"Look, I know you don't trust me right now, and you have no reason to, but I'm not doing this to harm you in any way."

"I can't imagine why you'd want to, so I'm willing to give you the benefit of the doubt. This situation is strange, as you put it, so you will forgive me if I'm on edge."

James inclined his head; he appreciated her candour, it actually relaxed him a little. "I know how you feel. None of this makes any sense to me, so I can't imagine what you must be thinking," he said.

Laura continued to watch him, but her gaze was less intense. "Why don't we start at the beginning and you can tell me what I'm doing here."

"If only it were that simple!"

"Isn't it?"

"Not at all, but I'll give it a go." James paused for a moment, trying to decide how to begin. "A few weeks ago, after the research I did on Donald Stacey for *Moment In Time*, I set to work with the intention of writing the article. I feel at this point I should explain a little about the way that I write, and I promise that you'll understand why I told you. There are different kinds of writers, in a broad sense, because we don't have all day; there are those who plan and those who don't. Ever since I was a boy, I could start a story, or piece of work with a small germ of an idea, and when I put pen to paper the instrument seemed to take on a life of its own. Before I knew it, I had written something I wasn't even aware I was feeling. I often joke that the writer inside me is another entity, who takes over my conscious thought as soon as I allow him to escape." James paused, trying to determine how she was feeling from her facial expression. "I realise what I'm telling you sounds a little odd and somewhat colourful, but please believe me when I tell you that I'm only trying to paint a picture so that you will understand what led me to publishing the letter."

"Mr. Pearson..."

"Call me James, please?"

"I understand that you want to make this as painless as possible, but I just want to know how the letters came into your hands. I have been waiting to find out since your call, and trust me when I say that I am not a patient person. Please just continue with your story and stop apologising for the way you are telling it!"

"You're right, of course. So, going back to the article I had been intending to write. I put pen to paper as I usually do, and began. When I looked back at what I had written, I was stunned. The letter, as you saw it printed, was there in front of me. At first I thought that it was an unconscious idea I had for a story, trying to find its way out. When I reread it, that explanation just didn't fit. I had other ideas but none of them seemed possible or even probable. The more letters I wrote, the more afraid I became."

"There are more letters?" Laura asked.

It threw James a little; he expected her to question the origin rather than the quantity. "Yes, I'll show them to you."

"And you're telling me that you wrote them?"

"Yes, that's what I'm telling you."

"How is that possible?" Laura asked. It felt like another reprimand; she seemed disappointed in the explanation.

"I don't know how it's possible, nor fully understand myself. I just know that the letters seemed to come to me for a reason, and I couldn't keep them to myself any longer."

"Let me get this straight. You believe you are being used as a vessel in some way?"

"That's exactly how it felt. I fought long and hard with the possibility. I am intuitive by nature, and you will understand this, excellent at reading body language…"

"I don't see what that has to do with the contents of the letter." Laura was caught up in the details.

"It's a process that I needed to go through. I'm an observant person, and can pick up things that many people miss. I get feelings about people. I guess what I'm trying to say is that I wondered if I had unconsciously picked up on certain things about you and they translated to paper."

Laura gave this some thought. "I never mentioned Matt's name."

"I realise that, but I also tend to remember facts that I read; piecing events together in my mind without even realising it."

"You think you read about us somewhere? That's a bit of a leap."

James couldn't help but smile. "I'm just trying to explain what I've been battling with and the reason I decided to print the letter."

"You said you would show me the others. May I see them?" Laura asked.

"Yes, I will go to arrange fresh coffee to give you a little time." James retrieved the letters from a folder on the desk, and passed them to her.

"Thank you," Laura answered. She didn't meet his gaze, even when he hesitated at the door.

When James returned to the room, Laura was silent for several moments. Without saying a word she gave him an elegant, leather bound journal. He noticed that all of the letters he had given her were sticking out like bookmarks, all pertaining to something important. He sat down and opened the journal at the first page, scanning the entry which Laura had penned. He compared her messages to the first letter, and continued until he had reached the last one. Each communication so obviously corresponded that it rendered James speechless. He touched Laura's delicate writing with his fingertips; the soft script seemed to mock him from the page. The words started to sway in front of his eyes; a sea of letters he wanted to wipe away rather than face their meaning. An image of a bridge flickered across his vision, startling him for a moment.

"After Matt died, I found it hard to continue with the day to day things. I was referred to a counsellor. During one of our sessions I acknowledged a longing to share my life with him again, just to be able to tell him the trivial things that I had taken for granted. My counsellor suggested a journal to record my thoughts and feelings; the letter format was my own idea." Laura paused for a moment, a faint smile curling the corners of her mouth. "Matt was right, I never expected to get a response, and if I had, it would not have been in quite this medium."

"So you think your husband is communicating to you from the grave?" James asked. He was shocked that she had reached this conclusion so readily.

"Don't you?"

"I don't know. I struggle to believe it, even now." James folded the journal and slid it across the table. "I think we both need time for this to sink in," he said. "Perhaps we can meet again to discuss where, if anywhere, we go from here."

Laura touched her journal thoughtfully. "Why don't you give me a call in a few days, and we can take it from there."

James smiled, understanding her caution. It was all a little much to take in. "I'll do that."

There didn't seem to be much to say after that. James was convinced she would think of a thousand questions as soon as she left the building, but at least she seemed more at ease. He walked her to the elevator, making small talk as they waited for it to arrive.

"Can I ask how your husband died?" James didn't know why it seemed so important.

"A group of college kids came off a bridge and landed on the dual carriageway below. It caused a pile up and…"

"I'm really sorry," James interrupted, he knew the rest.

"Thanks."

They were silent for a moment; each lost in their private thoughts. The bell to indicate the lift had arrived seemed deafening, but James was relieved all the same.

When he returned to the conference room, he sat for awhile, contemplating the possibility that he had been contacted by the 'spirit world' as mediums liked to call it. He realised something when Laura told him about her husband's death. He had been one of the reporters covering the story; nine people had lost their lives in the accident. James didn't remember seeing Matt's name in the list of fatalities, but it was a possibility. He was a little spooked by the image he had seen before Laura even mentioned the bridge, he didn't know what to make of that. James was certain of one thing, he couldn't sit in the room any longer, so he punched Barry's number into his phone and called in the cavalry; the time of day irrelevant.

Chapter Eleven

From: <u>Joanna@terpterp.org.uk</u>
To: Nicholas.carey@cfw.co.uk
Subject: Message from the dark side!

Hi Nicky

I missed a call from you today – how dare I be so important that I can't take a call from my best bud!

I hope your dad is feeling better; he was in fine spirits when I called yesterday and sending the nurses round the bend!

I'm really looking forward to next week. I can't believe it's been six months since our last sparring match.

On a serious note; have you heard from Laura? I'm sure you must have. What do you think to the letters? I'll call you tomorrow, if you let me know the best time.

See you soon, bud,
Love Jo xx

Nick frowned as he read the last paragraph of Jo's email. He had no idea what letters she referred to. It had been a few days since he'd last checked his emails, so there were twenty five new messages in his inbox; five of them were from Laura.

Thinking about it, Nick realised he hadn't spoken to Laura for awhile. She had sent numerous text messages; usually get well wishes for his father. He felt a pang of guilt that he hadn't made more of an effort; especially as she seemed to be trying so hard to reach him. He opened her first message, curious to discover what the fuss was all about.

From: lauraBSL@interpreter.co.uk
To: Nicholas.carey@cfw.co.uk
Subject: Sleep deprivation

Hi doc!

I'm sorry I didn't get a chance to see you again today. Jo called for lunch and we went to the hospital together. Mr. C looked rested, but it was still hard to see his large frame lying in a hospital bed. He always seemed like the man of steel when I was a kid, and I guess that's what he is – because your mum said he's doing really well.

Anyway, you are in my thoughts. If you need to talk, just ring me any time – day or night – my faithful friend insomnia is never too far away!

Hugs

Blue x

Smiling, Nick moved on to the next message.

From: lauraBSL@interpreter.co.uk

To: Nicholas.carey@cfw.co.uk

Subject: Is it a bird? Is it a plane? No, it's Mr. C!

I called in to see your dad again today. I'm flying to Dublin tonight for another theatre gig, so I'll try to catch you when I get back.

I can't believe how well he looks! Even your mum has stopped worrying so much. He really is amazing – like father like son. Speaking of my favourite Carey, (don't tell your dad) – how are you? Rebecca said you called in at the office, sorry I missed you.

Anyway, better pack – my script at least!

Take care, honey,
Love Laura x

Nick scanned through the next two; so far there was no mention of any letter. He opened the last one, hoping to solve the mystery.

From: lauraBSL@interpreter.co.uk
To: Nicholas.carey@cfw.co.uk
Subject: Communicating from the grave?

Hi Nick

I don't know if you're reading this before I've had a chance to speak to you. I wanted to call you tonight, but my mind is a mess and I don't know if you're working or not. I also didn't want you rushing over here because you have enough to worry about; namely your dad. I may make jokes about him being the 'man of steel', but I do it to try and show you that I care. We think our parents are invincible, and it can be quite a shock when we realise they're not.

I'm sorry, my thoughts are all over the place – I haven't even told you what I wanted to phone you about. I saw a letter earlier this evening that was printed in the Evening Post. The letter was addressed to me, and signed by Matt. Before you freak out, what I mean by that is his name was at the bottom of the message. As you can imagine, after the initial shock, I was furious because I thought someone was playing a practical joke. The strangest thing is, it seemed to be a reply to my journal entries – I will explain that to you when we speak. I just got off the phone with someone called James Pearson, and it turns out he published the letter. I don't really understand it yet, but I agreed to meet him.

I'm babbling now, so I'll sign off and try to get some sleep (who am I kidding?). I just feel so tired – the weary type that goes hand in hand with getting through the night on pure adrenalin.

Speak soon,
Love ya,
Blue x

Nick was so shocked by the words; he had to reread the email several times. He didn't even hear the nurse, as she tried to kick him off the computer.

"Hi, Stephanie," he answered distractedly, when she tapped his shoulder. "I'm finished, but I just need to use the phone. It won't take long." He logged out of his email account, and dialled Laura's mobile number. He felt hurt that she hadn't tried harder to speak to him about it; he had mentioned his PC at home was playing up.

"Hi, Nicky," Laura answered after the third ring. "Can you say it in ten words because I am just going in to an assignment?"

"Please tell me you're not going to meet the author of those bogus letters," Nick said before he could stop himself.

Laura tried to make light of the subject. "That's more than ten!"

"I'm not joking, Laura."

"Nick relax - I have already met James Pearson. He explained everything and I promise I will share it with you. He's really not a bad person."

"I can't believe you agreed to be in the same room as that freak. What possible explanation could he give?" Nick said. He realised his voice had gone up an octave, earning him a glance from Stephanie.

"I'm sorry, Nick, I have to go. Why don't you call and see me later and we can discuss it?"

"I...never mind; see you soon," Nick answered, mumbling his goodbye.

Stephanie was still looking at him with interest, probably hoping for a little gossip to discuss in the early hours. Nick smiled at her apologetically, knowing it was an unfair assumption. "Thanks, Steph. I suppose I should be going; my shift doesn't start for another three hours."

"Been visiting your dad?" she asked.

"Arguing with him more like - he wants to go home, so he isn't making life very easy on Ward 8."

"They'll cope," Stephanie said.

"I don't know if I will!"

Stephanie patted his arm. "Go let off some steam before you come back." She was distracted by some visitors who had approached the desk whilst they were talking.

"Thanks again, Steph," Nick said, taking his leave.

As he walked down into the main reception area, he decided to grab a coffee at the small café. It was predominantly used by visitors at the hospital but there was a small spattering of staff. Nick scanned his colleagues; he didn't feel like making small talk, or talking about his father. No-one seemed to notice him, and that suited him just fine.

His mind was full of his conversation with Laura. He knew he'd over reacted, but he was angry with her for being so foolish. For a fleeting moment he felt guilty that he'd given her a hard time. It wasn't fair of him to snap at her when she was about to go into a job. Laura told him often enough that she found it hard sometimes to leave her own 'baggage' at the door. Nick had mastered that art; it was almost like donning a new version of himself, every time he put on his scrubs. He prided himself on it; it wasn't always easy, but most of the time he managed just fine.

He moved down the queue, not paying attention to the people around him; he was lost in his own thoughts. When he felt a light tap on his shoulder, he turned in surprise.

"Hi, stranger," Samantha signed, throwing her arms around him before he could respond. Samantha was smaller than Laura, so she only came to his breast bone; it was almost like hugging a child. She reminded Nick of a small, delicate, china doll. Her features were smooth and porcelain like, a striking contrast to her dark hair.

"How are you?" Nick asked when she broke their embrace.

"Fine thanks. What about you? I heard about your dad."

Nick smiled at her. It was difficult to keep up sometimes; she was so fast. His BSL was far from perfect, but he was fluent enough to get by. Samantha, who was articulate and confident when using her first language, sometimes forgot that he struggled to follow at such speed.

He'd noticed over the years, that some deaf people adapted their use of the language when speaking to a hearing person. It was an automatic reaction, probably due to their past experiences and the number of communication difficulties they faced. Samantha made few exceptions for him; she did use a sign variety that was more English based. He enjoyed watching her, especially when she conversed with Laura. As sisters they had an informal, somewhat idiosyncratic style. Nick struggled to follow when they were in full flow, but he persevered because he did get parts of their conversation.

"He's tormenting all the nurses on his ward. When I left, he was trying to bribe them into getting him a drink," Nick said.

Samantha looked at him quizzically. "Your dad doesn't drink."

"Exactly! You can imagine what a nuisance he is, and all because he wants to go home."

"I'm sure the ward will seem boring when he's gone."

"Something like that! Anyway, what brings you to the hospital?" Nick asked her.

"I've been for a check up, that's all," Samantha replied. She didn't mention the purpose of her check up, so he didn't ask.

"I start in a few hours, so I thought I'd grab a coffee and chill for a while," he said instead.

"Do you have time to sit with me for ten minutes so we can catch up?" Samantha asked as they moved down the queue.

"I'd love to."

After being served, they found a vacant table and chatted for awhile. Nick noticed the curious glances from other visitors, and couldn't help smiling; it irritated Samantha when people stared. He accepted the attention because it helped to raise awareness; people sometimes called him the signing doctor, which he also accepted if it made them realise that everyone had a right to access information in their first language.

"Do you want to walk me out?" Samantha asked, cutting into his thoughts. Nick smiled in response, and stood up to accompany her.

When he said goodbye to Samantha, Nick decided he would visit the local sports centre for a game of squash. It was just what he needed to vent his frustrations – there would be plenty of volunteers. Not that they stood a chance, competing against him today.

Nick walked through the gates of Wentworth Park, and scanned the crowd. He was exhausted from working a double shift, but Charlie seemed upset when she rang, so he agreed to meet her. They had met for coffee a few days before, and spoken on the phone several times since. He enjoyed talking to her because she understood what he was going through. Nick usually turned to Laura, who knew exactly what to say; what he needed to hear. This time he felt unable to talk about his feelings and he didn't know why. Granted it had been Laura he called to see at the office, but then he bumped into Charlie and she helped him to rationalise his feelings in a way that no-one else could. He found himself wanting to talk to someone other than Jo or Laura about his father, so he contacted Charlie again.

Over the past couple of days he had almost called Laura a dozen times, but he still felt angry with her, which prevented him from actually picking up the phone. Nick knew he was being irrational, but he couldn't help it. With Charlie, he saw an opportunity to talk about himself; to hear a perspective that was different from his own.

Nick finally spotted her, and walked forwards with a smile. She hugged him briefly when he reached her. He noticed the dark circles under her eyes.

"I brought us some lunch. It's kind of late, I know, but I thought you might be hungry." Charlie indicated the bag at her feet.

Nick grinned. "I can eat at any time of the day. My father tells me I can eat for ten men!"

Without warning, Charlie burst into tears. It took them both by surprise and she wiped at her eyes ineffectually, embarrassed by the outburst.

"Hey, what is it?" he asked, putting an arm around her. "Come on; let's go down by the river. We can just sit, or you can talk." Nick scooped to pick up the food and guided her in the direction of the water.

"I'm sorry, Nick," Charlie said. She spoke so softly that he almost didn't hear her above the sound of the river.

"There's nothing to be sorry for."

"It's just that." Charlie took a deep breath to compose herself. "My dad found out that his cancer is back, and this time there is nothing they can do." This brought on another flood of tears; it was several minutes before she could speak. "It just seems so unfair, after all he's been through."

"I'm sorry, Charlie; that's tough," Nick said, rubbing her arm; he didn't know what else to say.

"Gary said we are lucky that we had the extra time with him, but I'm still so angry that we were allowed to hope. I can't seem to get past that."

"What you're feeling is perfectly natural. You may be grateful one day, you may not. Right now, you have to deal with this the best way you can," Nick said.

"I'm not dealing with it very well at all. Gary wants me to go up to Scotland and help him set up the new house, but all I want to do is spend every waking moment with my dad. It feels like every minute could be the last one, and I don't have enough of them. I feel detached from everything and everyone, even my husband. I'm trying so hard to see this from his point of view. I know he loves dad, but right now I feel too sensitive about everything. I can't even talk about it without breaking down."

"If you want to spend time with your father, then do it - I'm sure Gary will understand if other things take a back seat for awhile." Nick wanted to help, but he knew that aside from being a shoulder to cry on, there was nothing he could do. He could only imagine what she was going through; he was still coming to terms with his father's scare.

They sat for a time, occasionally talking, but mostly in a comfortable silence as they ate. Nick had to leave eventually because the fatigue had set in and he could barely function. When he left the park, he made Charlie promise to ring him if she needed to talk. He knew she had a lot to think about, as well as talk through, but she would have to do it in her own time. He was a little uncomfortable talking about the problems within her marriage. He didn't know Gary, so he didn't think it was fair to analyse or discuss their future out of context. It also made him too aware of their growing friendship. It didn't feel like they were doing anything wrong, but he knew that he had to be careful because Charlie was vulnerable and he didn't want her to get hurt.

Chapter Twelve

Dear Matt

It feels strange writing this letter, almost like someone is looking over my shoulder! It is mind blowing that my messages actually reached you, whether they were written that way or not. I can't decide if you are here with me, watching me try to form coherent thoughts on paper, or whether you are 'reading my diary' after the event. Either one of those makes me feel like I should be taking medication! Seriously, it is all a little surreal.

One thing I'm sure of is that I feel really close to you right now. Even though the previous entries were therapeutic in their own way, this is the most benefit I've had since I started. I know I'm not being very clear, but you always did have a way of seeing past my muddled thoughts and deciphering the meaning.

I'd better leave it there, before any cohesion in this letter starts to fall apart.

Until the next time my love,
Laura x

Laura closed her journal and placed it back in the desk drawer. It had taken her a week to write it. She had missed seven days worth of entries; a feat in itself. It took her that long to come to terms with the revelations in her meeting with James Pearson. He was a strange one, his sensitivity and self conscious humour had taken her by surprise.

She thought about their first meeting, when he had spouted some cheesy line about taking her out, and realised that he had been full of the same nervous energy. She had simply misinterpreted his eagerness for arrogance. It was ironic really; she was usually good at reading people. Still, having been given the chance to observe him in a different situation, she had to admit that he had a certain charm. He was tall and long-limbed, with a mop of sandy coloured hair, and eyes that sparkled with character. He was attractive, even more so because of his self assured posture. Laura got the impression he rarely became as tongue tied as he had on that day; it was flattering in a way.

She hadn't talked to anyone about James. Sam and Jo had been on the phone the moment she left the meeting; Jo from somewhere in the south having returned to her busy schedule, and her sister through Typetalk, a national relay service. She had promised to explain everything when she had digested the information herself. Telling Nick had been a little more difficult. Laura hadn't seen him in almost two weeks; if she was a paranoid person she would think he was avoiding her. Every time she tried to reach him he was nowhere to be found, and he had missed their weekly rendezvous for two weeks in a row. All of which made it hard to share her news with her best friend.

During one telephone call she tried to broach the subject, but he thought she was crazy for meeting James in the first place. He didn't ask how it went, so she didn't tell him. Laura hoped they would be able to clear things up later that evening. It was her mother and father's wedding anniversary and they were having a party to celebrate the milestone. Nick was present at most family gatherings.

She wondered briefly what time he would arrive - she didn't want to get there too early because she found family occasions tiring at the best of times. She loved her family, and in smaller groups she had a ball, but during the larger gatherings she usually hid in a corner with Nick. They had always been that way; observing from a distance, and generally amusing themselves. By now they were pros at blending in; sitting near the food usually did the trick. These thoughts led to Matt; he had loved family events and had darted from person to person catching up on their lives, leaving Laura to cause mischief with her friend. Jo on the other hand, avoided parties like the plague. She came, stayed an hour at the outside and left in a flurry of apologies that she couldn't stay longer.

Laura rummaged through her wardrobe, to find a suitable outfit. It was a family tradition to look one's best when celebrating; she had loved dressing up as a child. On special occasions their 'best clothes' came out and Laura felt it added to the festivities, the fact that everyone made an effort.

She made her choice, and laid it out on the bed. As she walked to take a shower, Laura had a spring in her step. She didn't know how this next chapter in her life would pan out, and part of her was afraid of what came next, but she hadn't felt as positive in a long time.

Laura was sandwiched between her father's brothers when Nick arrived at the party; she quickly made her excuses, before lunging at her friend in relief.

"Hi, sweetie; where've you been hiding?" she asked as he hugged her back.

"Nowhere special. I've been kind of busy."

As they walked to a quieter side of the house, Laura observed her friend with amusement. Nick looked more like he belonged on the big screen than behind a surgeons mask. He was a bear of a man; the black jumper he was wearing accentuated his athletic body. Laura knew he would be embarrassed by her observations. But like it or not, with thick black hair and crystal blue eyes; he was a catch for any women, all 6ft 2in of him.

"What are you thinking? You have that twinkle in your eye," Nick asked her.

"I was just thinking how scrumptious you look tonight. You could have any bedside manner you wanted, and still make most of your patients happy!"

Nick held out a chair for her. "Oh, so you're in one of those moods tonight." He ruffled her hair like he had done when they were younger and she was being 'a girl'

"Watch it, Carey!"

"What kind of a word is scrumptious anyway? I feel like something edible."

"Oh sorry, Mr. 'Me Tarzan, You Jane,' what would you prefer?"

Nick grinned. "Distinguished will do, or you could try handsome, dishy, attractive, good looking - that kind of thing."

"No, scrumptious is the perfect word. It's a girl thing; if you look it up in a dictionary, one of the meanings is attractive," Laura told him. She marvelled at the utter rubbish they could spout.

"Look, I'm worried about this obsession you have with me, it could ruin a perfectly good friendship," Nick said, edging his chair a littler further away from hers.

"You're right - I will try to control myself!" Laura giggled at his expression. "Seriously though, you look great."

"Thank you, I feel good; better than I've done in weeks."

Laura nodded, knowing how hard his Dad's illness was on him.

"Hey, Mrs. K," Nick signed to Catherine, Laura's mum, as she came over, interrupting the conversation.

Catherine laughed and planted a kiss on his cheek. Names were not used in this way in sign language; they were usually reserved for introductions. When a person was known to you, a simple greeting would do. Nick was aware of this cultural difference, but he knew it entertained Catherine.

"Hello, you look very handsome this evening."

"Thank you. Have a word with your daughter, she uses words like scrumptious," Nick said, fingerspelling 'scrumptious' because he didn't know what else to do. Catherine looked at her daughter quizzically, not familiar with the word. Laura translated; making her mum laugh.

"Like mother, like daughter!" Nick said rolling his eyes.

"You two are as bad as each other, so don't drag me into it," Catherine said. "I like the word though, it suits you."

Nick pulled a face; he knew he couldn't win. Laura had inherited her playful side from her mother. "I honestly don't know what you mean, we are very well behaved."

"That's because you hide. I suspect most of the trouble starts with you two at the centre of it."

Laura laughed at Nick's expression; he portrayed the picture of innocence. She enjoyed the banter between them; Nick liked teasing her mother, and she wouldn't have it any other way.

"Well, tonight we'll be on our best behaviour. You can trust me, I'm a surgeon!" Nick said.

"And I'm her daughter – that should earn me a few brownie points!"

"As I said, you two are as bad as each other," Catherine replied. "I don't know what to do with you."

Laura grinned, resisting the urge to make a joke. Nick must have sensed this, because he shook his head in silent agreement.

"Anyway, I have other guests, so I'll catch up with you soon. The food table is usually the best place to find you anyway."

"Have fun," Nick said, growing serious for a moment. "Congratulations on your wedding anniversary."

"Thanks."

Laura jumped up to kiss her mum on the cheek. She was a skilled hostess, so it would probably be some time before they got chance to speak again. She looked across the room and marvelled at the number of people they could cram into a three-bedroom detached. It was fortunate that her father had taken up DIY since retiring. The dining room and lounge were now one big open space, which was perfect for entertaining. The conservatory, where they were sat, could hold a fair sized buffet table, so guests didn't have to spend half the night dodging the queue as it weaved across the room.

"So," Nick said, as Catherine moved on to her other guests. "When are you going to tell me about your meeting with the 'letter' guy?"

"His name is James Pearson," Laura said, unusually irritated by his tone.

"I don't care what his name is!" Nick snapped. The force of his words took them both by surprise.

"What's going on with us? I've never waited for you to ask about something important in my life, ever. I didn't bring it up because you didn't ask and let's face it, we haven't seen much of each other lately," Laura said. They'd had plenty of arguments growing up, and never held it against each other. This felt different somehow; they were in unfamiliar territory.

Nick sighed heavily. "I know. Maybe I'm being over protective; I just can't help feeling that this whole thing will come between us."

"Why should it?

"I don't know, Blue. I guess I just don't see what you have to gain by drudging up old feelings of loss."

"Well maybe you don't know me as well as you think, or you haven't been paying attention, because there is nothing to drudge up. The loss is as big a part of my life as breathing; I'm just trying to get through it and maybe somehow James can help."

"What about the rest of us? The ones who should be able to make a difference, not some stranger with an ulterior motive." Nick was clearly angry; she could see it in the tense lines of his body. His eyes were a darker shade of blue; another telltale sign. For a moment, Laura didn't know how to respond; she had no idea he felt so strongly about it. They had not discussed the letters or her contact with James Pearson in any detail.

"Nicky, you are one of the most important people in my life…"

"Don't patronise me, Laura. If you think I'm looking for reassurance, you're missing the point."

"I am missing the point. All I wanted was to discuss something important to me with my best friend," Laura said sadly.

"I know. I'm sorry."

She waited, but he didn't say anything else, or encourage her to continue. Laura attempted humour. "I'll tell you about it another time. We don't want to start a fight at the party, you know what mum said!"

"If I remember correctly, it was your father who started the food fight last year," Nick said, consenting to let their disagreement drop.

Laura smiled at the memory. Her father had been a little drunk and threw a cherry from the top of the trifle at his brother, who was in the process of telling some embarrassing story about their childhood. Victor retaliated by returning fire with the already weeping cherry and missed the target. It sailed straight past his brother and landed with artistic flare on Aunt Jemima's white blouse. The fighting ended there. She made them both eat humble pie and pay for her dry cleaning bill to boot; it had been one of the funniest things Laura had witnessed.

"What are you two up to?" Samantha asked as she approached the buffet table and popped a sausage roll into her mouth.

At any family function in the Kane household there was an unspoken rule that BSL was used. Laura's parents tried to integrate the two worlds and accepted that hearing culture was also a part of their lives; they understood that Laura needed to relax and use her first language when no Deaf people were involved in the conversation.

"Just contemplating whether we should spice things up a little," Laura said.

Nick stood up to hug Samantha. "Actually, you will have to do it without me. I need to get going."

"That's a shame," Samantha replied, stealing his seat.

Laura said nothing; she was wondering why he suddenly had to leave. It would make him the first to go, when he was usually the last. He looked at her briefly, but averted his gaze a little too quickly.

"I promised a colleague I would help out with something," Nick said. "I'll catch up with you later."

"You never mentioned you had to leave early." Laura had the distinct impression that he was leaving to avoid further confrontation; he had never backed down before.

"Sorry, I'll make it up to you all," Nick replied, placing a kiss on Laura's cheek, before disappearing to begin his round of goodbyes. It was one of the things Laura loved about Deaf culture, the sense of community. It just took half the night to get through all the farewells, whenever there was a meeting of friends and family alike.

Laura watched Nick trying to squeeze out of her Aunt's embrace, and missed him terribly. It was an odd feeling, but it felt like she was losing his friendship. He didn't look back at her as he left the room and this compounded Laura's feelings of dread; he would normally pull a funny face or wink whilst tipping an imaginary hat. She didn't know why, but Nick was distancing himself from her.

The Guardian rode next to Laura as she drove home. He was thinking about the fragility of the human spirit. He didn't fully understand why people were so reluctant to say what was in their heart. He suspected that fear was high on the list; creatures of habit, so many people were ruled by their emotions.

It was unfathomable to him that the ones, who expressed themselves from the heart, without giving thought to the consequences, were often ridiculed because of a mysterious code of behaviour. It seemed common practice to listen to those inner demons. The Guardian was overcome by a compulsion to ask Laura why she couldn't share her insecurities with Nick. As close as they were and as much as they shared, sometimes they could be as distant as strangers.

He didn't doubt that nature was a beautiful and powerful force. Part of what made the Guardian's job so special, was the ability to nurture and guide a soul through life. The danger, as he saw it, was in situations manufactured by humankind; there was often cruelty, either enforced or perceived, without a mechanism to correct itself. The Guardian had cradled souls during his time on earth, who were in a considerable amount of pain, either physically or psychologically; he was with them every step of the way.

He glanced across at Laura in the driver's seat. She had not slept well recently and he was concerned about her ability to fight the fatigue now invading her body. Laura was a conscientious person; she often pulled over to the side of the road to rest before continuing her journey. Tonight she was preoccupied, so he watched her more closely in case she needed a little help to stay awake.

Chapter Thirteen

```
To: Nicky
Hi hon. I missed you again this week...I haven't watched
a good film in ages. It is not the same without you
to share it with – I have nobody to tease me for not
following the plot! Call me...I feel like I lost my
good arm and my brain does not function without it!
Call me, damn you! Blue x x
```

Laura sat at her desk, a smile lingering on her face as she thought of her younger sister's boyfriend Harry. She had spoken to him only moments ago, and as usual his energy was contagious. So much so that she now found herself humming as she worked. Harry contacted her to talk about a surprise party he was planning for Monica's eighteenth birthday, but the conversation somehow turned to Nick; Laura found herself sharing her fears with him

Harry was an amazing young man; everyone who knew him adored him. At seventeen he was more mature than most boys his age. He doted on Monica, would do anything for her, and had been doing since his family moved next door to their parents, seven years ago. Harry had visited the office a few times; his loveable nature and wicked sense of humour had boosted morale and earned him even more admirers. It was Harry who initiated the term 'Chief'; her colleagues had been annoying her with it ever since.

He reminded her of Nick in many ways, this was perhaps one of the reasons she found him so easy to talk to. His wacky expressions were a part of what made him so much fun, it was never boring when he was around.

Laura turned at the sound of a knock on her office. "Come in," she called, smiling as Charlie popped her head around the door.

"Hi, Charlie."

"Hi, Laura, can I have a word in private please?"

Laura nodded her agreement, realising she hadn't seen her in weeks. She motioned for her to take a seat. "Of course."

Charlie entered the room and closed the door behind her. On closer inspection Laura was shocked at how tired she looked.

"I have a problem I'm hoping you can help me with," Charlie said.

"I'll certainly try."

"My trip to Scotland has been postponed; things are a little crazy at the moment. I wondered if you would allow me to stay on for awhile - I need to keep busy," Charlie asked; her face gave nothing away.

Laura was shocked into silence; she had no idea Charlie was having problems. "Oh, honey. I'm so sorry we haven't had an opportunity to chat recently. Of course you can stay on. Has the move been postponed long?"

"No, Gary is still going. I'm staying behind for a while until he sets things up."

Laura looked at her friend and colleague, she wanted to help her through this difficult time, but Charlie was not willing to say more, and she didn't want to pry. Laura had known her a long time, so she knew the defensive move was Charlie's way of coping.

"It will be great to hold onto you a little longer," Laura told her. She didn't want to make Charlie uncomfortable. If she wanted to say more she would do so in her own time.

"Thanks, Laura. I appreciate it."

"I don't need your gratitude. You are a valued member of the team and…" Laura was interrupted by the sound of her mobile phone. "Sorry, hon. I will just switch that off." Laura began rummaging through her bag.

"No, answer it. I have a job anyway," Charlie said. She was already on her feet.

She was about to object when she noticed it was Nick. She looked up to apologise for the intrusion, but Charlie had already gone. She didn't have time to dwell on her hasty exit.

"Hey, doc!" she smiled into the receiver.

"Hi, Blue. As you probably gathered, I got your message." Laura could hear the smile in Nick's voice.

"What are you up to?" Laura asked

"I'm just grabbing a sandwich to keep the old energy levels up."

"Thanks for calling. I didn't mean to be a drama queen!"

"Yes, you did, but that's okay. I feel suitably chastised for my foul mood of late. Can I call and see you tomorrow night?" Nick asked.

"I'd love that. Do you fancy a take away and a movie?"

"Maybe a take away, but the movie will have to wait. I need to talk to you about something," Nick sounded a little distracted by something going on in the background.

"No problem. Now go save some lives!"

Nick laughed. "I'll try."

Laura sat back in her chair and closed her eyes for a moment. She was worried about Charlie, and she didn't know what to do about it. One thing was clear, as she tried to concentrate on her work, she wouldn't get anything done brooding about it. Laura decided to go in search of company; she was happy to find David and Duncan in the office.

"Hi, you two, I'm not interrupting any male bonding am I?" Laura asked.

"Just debriefing," David said, jumping to his feet. "How about a coffee?"

"Good, because I'm going out for lunch," Becky called from her office, making Laura laugh.

"Don't let her make you think that I'm a tyrant and expect coffee in my hand every time I move," Laura said to Duncan.

"I've already seen how efficient she is. But you are our commander and chief!"

"Not you already, I thought that you would bring a level of sensibility to the place," Laura said, feigning exasperation.

David had located Laura's mug from her office, and now turned to Duncan. "Can I get you a coffee, D?"

"Why not, I should just get an intravenous drip - it would be so much easier!"

"I knew there was a reason we agreed to give you that contract," Laura agreed. "Is it interpreters in general who are addicted to coffee or did I just get lucky?"

"I think you just got lucky."

"How goes your first week?" Laura asked him. She liked his casual style and confident air. He looked like a college professor, and his eccentric personality was endearing.

"It's been great. The team are everything you said they would be and more; they answer my questions before I even ask them."

"I'm glad you're enjoying it."

"David and Phoebe are priceless! I don't know how any work gets done," he said; completely aware that David was on his way back with the coffee.

"I've been telling Laura for years that Phoebe is a bad influence."

"Speaking of Phoebe, she has been working on the video suite for the past couple of days. We should take a look and perhaps test the system, especially as we are extending the service to videophone interpreting," Laura suggested.

Duncan clapped his hands together. "Sounds like fun. I'm interested in taking a peek. I've used some pretty poor equipment in the past, so I have a little experience I could pass on."

"That would be useful. It's the first time we've used the service properly. The whole team went on a training day, and certain issues were raised that you could perhaps help out with."

"I am terrified about using the system. I know it will save time and is good in terms of access for Deaf people, but the reception concerns me," David said. It had taken Laura quite a while to convince him it was a good thing.

"Why don't we see if the room is available now? We can have a quick look whilst drinking unlimited cups of coffee and maybe play with the equipment a little?" Duncan suggested.

Laura smiled, pleased that at least one member of the team had interpreted via videophone before.

The room had taken a lot of time to set up; visual noise had to be taken into account, as well as, lighting, direction, background and compatibility. Phoebe had put a lot of work into it.

"I think that's an excellent idea," she told them, glancing at her watch. "I have a meeting in one hour, but I'm all yours till then!"

"An offer only one of us can refuse," David replied cheekily, making Laura choke on her coffee.

Duncan gave her a pat on the back. "You walked into that one."

"I swear I do it on purpose, just to spice up his material!"

Laura followed them out of the office, thinking how lucky she was to be part of such a good team. She often wondered if she picked people at interview that had the same sort of principles. Every member of the team was passionate about their job, and though they spent most of their 'down time' fooling around, they were a professional, hard-working group - one which Laura was proud to belong to.

Chapter Fourteen

```
From: Nicky
Hi Blue. Sorry but I can't make it tomorrow - I have
to work. I will give you a bell later and we can catch
up then x
```

Laura checked her reflection in the rear-view mirror one last time before getting out of the car. She didn't know why her appearance was so important, it was only the second time she'd met James Pearson face to face. Laura couldn't deny that there was something about him that she felt drawn to; it was more than just a connection to Matt. They had spoken on the phone several times.

The first time she agreed to meet James, she was convinced she would dislike him. For a brief moment, when she realised they had met before, she almost called an end to their meeting. She was glad that she'd seen in through because a strange thing happened; she actually liked him.

Their initial encounter was unfortunate, because it had been a particularly bad day; she had dismissed James at the time as being an insensitive jerk. When she reflected on her reaction now, she realised that she had vented her frustrations on him because she had secretly enjoyed his over familiar, yet playful banter.

She locked the car, and scanned the group of people outside her favourite restaurant. Laura spotted James immediately; she couldn't prevent the laugh that escaped when she saw the huge grin on his face.

It had been her idea to meet at the restaurant; she wanted a more informal setting for their second meeting.

"Hi, Laura," James said, as she approached.

"Hi, yourself".

"I took the liberty of ordering a table. I know it isn't a weekend but it's pretty full in there." He steered her towards the door.

"I have good taste, but it comes at a price! We will probably be waiting awhile." Laura instantly wished she had booked in advance; she wasn't very good at remembering the details unless she wrote them down. Laura's 'to do' lists were legendary; Nick teased her mercilessly about the fact that she forgot birthdays unless he reminded her.

Laura followed James into the restaurant. She allowed him to take her coat and hand it to an attendant, who swapped the garment for a ticket stub. As they walked into the bar, Laura turned to James. "Should we get a drink whilst we are waiting?"

"Good idea, what can I get you?"

"Dry white wine, please." She had been about to insist on buying her own, but something about the way he asked made her bite her tongue.

They managed to find a seat, which was lucky considering the number of people crowded into the bar area. Laura soon began to relax into their conversation. She couldn't deny they had a connection; she felt it during their recent telephone conversations.

Laura was intrigued by James's recent confession that the letters made him question his beliefs. She was an idealist; she believed that any God would accept the limitations of a human soul, without unnecessary restrictions. She didn't believe that was merely a convenient way of securing her ticket into heaven without following the rules, neither a preferable option to having no belief system at all, but she did have an open mind when it came to spirituality. Laura's faith was about believing in something beyond her mortal self, derived from the power of the human spirit.

For James who was analytical by nature, this uncertainty was not enough. He needed cold hard facts before he could accept something he did not understand. He had lost any faith he had long ago. Despite being sceptical of a higher being, James was willing to consider the possibilities that presented themselves. He still suspected that his unconscious had instigated their second meeting, but she didn't fully understand the logic behind that.

"What are you thinking about?" James asked, bringing her back to their conversation; her mind had been far away.

"The forces behind the reason we met."

"I definitely think our meeting was orchestrated in some way, though I think we would have met with or without the forces you talk about. I hate knowing that without having an explanation for it; it contradicts my view of fate or destiny. I thought we made our own. This though, what is happening to us, feels extraordinarily like someone is encouraging us down this particular path."

"Why not stop torturing yourself and let what will be, be. This new found friendship we have; be it luck, serendipity, a freak of nature..."

James laughed at that, his eyes twinkling in merriment. "I'll drink to that," he said raising his glass.

Laura raised her own and let the delicate crystal connect with his. She liked the way it sounded.

"Cheers," she said, taking a sip of her wine.

As she did so, she let her eyes drift briefly across the room. Laura hadn't taken in her surroundings until now; she was surprised by the number of people squashed into the dining area. The restaurant had grown in popularity, so much so, that they were obviously struggling to cope with the numbers.

"I think we may have to sit outside!" James said, following her gaze.

Laura nearly choked on her wine. It wasn't the comment that had caused the sharp intake of breath; it was the couple she spotted across the room. James jumped up from his chair and appeared at her side in a flash. It took Laura a moment to get her breath back; she was so shocked to see Nick and Charlie that for a moment all she could concentrate on was them. When James began patting her back, he drew attention from the other diners; it was too late to avoid Nick's inquisitive glance. When their eyes met, Laura felt the jolt of his surprise like a physical blow; he could not hide the guilt, even from a distance.

"Are you all right?" James asked with concern.

"I..." Laura didn't know what to say. She was being controlled by such powerful emotions that every fibre of her being wanted to be anywhere but in this room.

"James," she said, turning her attention back to him. "This is going to sound like a scene from a really bad play, but I need to go."

James scanned the room questioningly; his eyes seeking anything out of the ordinary, before coming back to rest on her. "Of course, I'll get our coats," he said, immediately moving to pull out her chair.

"I'll come with you." Laura rose quickly, holding the arm he offered to steady herself. "Thank you, James."

"Laura, what a pleasant surprise," Nick said, making her jump.

The anger that had been battling inside her rose to the surface as she whirled to face him. "I doubt that, Nick."

"Laura?" She saw the confusion on James's face; he raised an eye brow, looking from Laura to Nick and back again.

"It isn't what you're thinking. Come on, Blue, be reasonable for a moment," Nick said.

"James and I were just leaving," Laura answered tightly. She turned away from her friend and marched past a bewildered James.

"If you don't mind giving us a moment," Nick said; it came out more like a command than a request.

He caught up with her at the coat room. Laura was frantically searching through her bag for the ticket; it was a familiar sight.

"Laura, just listen to me for a moment," Nick said, he sounded anxious.

"We've been friends for a long time, so you should know that when I'm upset about something, following me like you did in infant school is not a good idea," Laura said. She glanced over his shoulder, and noticed James a few paces behind him.

"Fine, if that's how you want to do this, I'll take Charlie home and meet you at the apartment." Nick turned on his heel and left, leaving no room for negotiation.

Laura was so angry she wanted to scream, but instead she looked towards James. "I'm so sorry about this," she said. It was not how she anticipated their evening. "Can we start this evening again, or as the Americans would say 'take a rain check'?" she asked, embarrassed by the scene she had caused.

"No problem. Do you want me to take you home?"

"I'll be fine, but I feel terrible about this."

"Don't worry, like you said, we can do it another time. I don't really understand what is going on, but I hope you get it straightened out. Call me if you need to talk." James was shuffling his weight from one foot to the other like a child. Laura smiled at him, he was a nice man and she found his shyness around her charming.

"Thanks, I appreciate that." She began to rummage through her bag again. This time plucking her cloakroom ticket from its depths and waving it triumphantly.

"Here, allow me," James said, moving to collect her coat.

The attendants were more efficient, and James had her jacket in his hand a few moments later. He helped her to shrug it on, and escorted her to her car. Laura wondered what he was thinking. Now that she had time to reflect, she realised that she had over-reacted and felt like a fool.

The Guardian walked beside Laura, matching her step for step. She had been pacing impatiently in her flat for forty minutes; walking in the same spot so often she created a slight indentation in the carpet. She would occasionally stop her ritual to stare wistfully at a photograph of Nick on her fireplace. It was a graduation shot; Nick looked young and carefree. The Guardian remembered he had been goading Laura about something; he had the same expression on his face he had been carrying since they were children. It is one of Laura's favourite photographs, though at the moment it seemed to be the cause of her anxiety.

The Guardian was convinced there were moments when she sensed his presence; she had stopped walking a few times and each time coincided with his efforts to comfort her. He was fascinated by the fact that when he put his hand in hers or placed it gently on her shoulder, her attention would return to the snapshot of Nick. Had she felt safe on that day? Was it a time in her life that she could look back on and gain perspective?

He knew that Laura mapped out many happy events from her life in memory albums. He often watched her draw the pages together with care, wondering at her ability to relive every moment as she did so. Nick was an important part of that, she often joked that he was from the same pod. The Guardian sensed her fear that their relationship was changing beyond her control.

It was at times like these, watching her confusion that he grew concerned about his plan. Sometimes, his interventions, no matter how small, were more of a hindrance. He tried not to question; happy that he didn't have the power to change events or impart his own views. He would not welcome the responsibility. Whatever happened tonight was out of his control. He could not help Laura with the decisions she was about to make, because he would be influencing her without agreement or justification.

The Guardian knew that people often prayed for answers to their questions, not even sure who they were seeking help from. It was more about a need for reassurance so that part of the responsibility could be taken away. In reality they would not welcome such interference if they had a choice. He was also aware that many people struggled with difficult decisions; it would be easier for them to turn over some element of control, but how often would someone knowingly trust another with this kind of power?

The Guardian had no choice but to stand by and allow events to unravel; he would be there for Laura, to support her, each step of the way.

Laura flinched when she heard the knock, though she had been expecting it. She hesitated slightly before she crossed the small distance to open the door.

"Come in," she said, standing aside when he made no attempt to enter.

"I see you've calmed down."

Laura felt the fight drain from her body. "Nick, please don't goad me because you don't want to deal with this situation."

"You're right. For the first time in my life I want to turn away and tell you this is none of your business. I can't explain that, I just know that I'm angry. The biggest part is because you made me feel like I've done something to offend your precious principles." Nick was now pacing in almost the same place Laura had just vacated.

"I'm sorry you feel that way. If you don't want to tell me about it then don't, but I saw your expression Nick, and I know how you were feeling when you saw me in the restaurant," Laura said quietly.

"That's the problem though, perhaps the real problem. You think you can interpret the way I'm feeling, but the sad truth is that you can't."

"What exactly do you mean by that?" Laura asked him. She was surprised how level her voice sounded.

Nick was visibly angry; she could see his jaw clenching as he struggled to control it. "What you thought you saw was misinterpreted;

it had nothing to do with who I was with or any of the other things running through your head."

Laura stared at him, taken aback. His anger had never been focused on her with such passion before. "That was unfair and you know it. I have nothing to gain from this situation, whether I misunderstood it or not. It's interesting how you know what's going through my head, yet I'm not allowed to guess what's going through yours."

Nick sighed in frustration. He stopped pacing and regarded her thoughtfully. "This is getting us nowhere. I will accept that we know each other very well, perhaps better than most people. But maybe we should try to forget that and have a conversation without our history being an obstacle," Nick said.

"I think that's impossible, given that you are not willing to answer my questions." Laura sat back on the couch and let her head rest against the cushion; she was exhausted.

"We need to sort this out before it comes between us. Ask your questions and I will try to answer them."

Laura looked at him sadly. He may not want to admit it, but she knew him well enough to know that he had no intention of answering her questions. "Are you the reason Charlie is staying, instead of joining her husband as planned?" she asked, knowing her directness would not surprise him.

"I suppose you used the word 'husband' for dramatic effect. Are you adding insult to injury and accusing me of having an affair?"

"I didn't accuse you of anything. I know you wouldn't do that unless you were in a situation…"

"Damn you, Laura," Nick said, cutting her off. "Damn you for not understanding that I might want to confide in someone other than you, damn you for jumping to conclusions and damn you for being so obsessed with your dead husband that you need to find a substitute to keep him alive."

She could tell that Nick instantly regretted his outburst; the blood drained from his face when he realised what he had said.

"Please leave," Laura whispered. Her voice was raw from the emotions she was suppressing.

Nick didn't move. His eyes begged her to reconsider.

"I said, get out." This time the full force of Laura's anger hit him head on. He didn't say anything further; he merely walked the small distance to the door, and let himself out.

Laura felt bereft. The tears she had been holding in check flowed openly now; they wouldn't stop. All the tension, all the uncertainty of the past couple of weeks, had finally come to a head; it felt as though she had lost something she would never get back. She was scared, because in all the years of friendship, they had never let something as trivial come between them. She didn't understand why it was happening; she had laughed at the people who told her their friendship wouldn't last. Laura had been told many times that their partners would not understand the bond they shared and it would drive a wedge between them. Yet, even when she married Matt, and Nick met Zoe, they had maintained their relationship because it seemed as important to them as breathing. Matt never questioned what they had; he understood completely her need to have Nick in her life. Now, after all this time, something which Lara could not explain had torn them apart and perhaps proven their cynics right all along.

Laura was certain of only one thing; Nick was keeping something from her, something big. It was the reason for her over-reaction. She had practically accused him of breaking up a marriage, and she felt bad about that. There was something she was missing, something she needed to figure out before it was too late.

Chapter Fifteen

To: lauraBSL@interpreter.co.uk

From: Nicholas.Carey@cfwl.co.uk

Laura

I feel dreadful about our argument, disagreement, falling out or whatever you want to call it. Sometimes I wish we were still in first grade so that I could offer you some of my milk, and pull a face, and you'd know how sorry I am.

Let's talk at the party?

Doc xx

Nick willed the sounds of the operating theatre to wash over him. He was struggling to focus and could feel his concentration slipping away. This was usually his sanctuary; nothing could penetrate the work he did in this room. He relied on his ability to disassociate himself from Nick the 'person' and become only the doctor; everything he had, concentrated on his task. It was failing him today; just when he started to relax he was side tracked by an image he had no right to see when he was working.

Nick glanced at his colleague, hoping that Ted would understand his moment of weakness. "Could you close?" he asked, ignoring the surprised look on Ted's face.

"Sure, Dr. Carey."

They had been operating for just under an hour; it was a routine appendectomy and Ted was more than capable of completing the procedure. Nick didn't immediately leave the theatre, even though the lights seemed too bright and the hum of machinery too loud. He hated himself at that moment for allowing his personal life to interfere with his work.

As he observed his colleague, Nick allowed himself to think about the reason for his mental torture. He found it difficult to admit, but after everything that had happened over the past couple of weeks, he needed a break. His argument with Laura had tipped him over the edge; he could still feel the anger that had erupted in him last night.

Nick had always known his feelings for Laura would cause a problem in their relationship eventually. He had been trying to convince himself that their friendship was enough for him, most of his adult life. His ex-wife had known that he could never truly love anyone as much as he loved Laura. It wasn't the only thing wrong with their relationship, but it hadn't helped. When she announced she was moving away last year, he hadn't put up much of a fight. Nick regretted hurting her, no matter how volatile their marriage had been. Zoe would never forgive him for his part in the divorce; she had sent her best wishes to his mother, but she hadn't been to visit since his father became ill.

As for Laura, she didn't suspect a thing and that hurt more than he was willing to admit. It also frustrated him that she couldn't see what was staring her in the face. Nick had a stubborn streak, which occasionally clouded his judgement; part of him didn't want to tell Laura what she should have known instinctively. It wasn't fair, but he didn't care. He didn't understand how she could look into his eyes and know so much about him, know exactly how he felt, but miss the depth of his feelings for her. He felt like *Clark Kent* in the early years; he could never understand how *Lois Lane* could look at *Clark* and not see the man she was in love with staring her straight in the face. If he could get his head around that, he could then figure out why his friend could look into his soul, yet not see how he truly felt.

With a heavy sigh, Nick removed his surgical mask, and followed Ted out of the theatre. They stood silently at the sink for a moment, as they cleaned up.

"Is something bothering you Nick?" Ted asked, breaking the silence.

"I'm fine. I think it's time for that vacation I've been promising myself," Nick said. They weren't particularly close, but he respected Ted and knew he could count on his support.

"I can't remember the last time you took a holiday. Then again, it isn't always easy when we feel duty bound to our patients."

"Tell me about it."

"It would be the most sensible thing to do though Nick. As your friend and colleague, I've seen the recent strain you've been under."

Nick smiled at that. "And here I was thinking I am Mr. Cool!"

"That's a reputation you can save for the med students! You don't have to pretend to be super human; you're a good man, but even you need a break."

"You've talked me into it, Ted!" Nick said, teasing him a little. In truth he felt a new found respect for his colleague.

"Johnson is practically packing my suitcase for me. You spend all your time fighting for a break in the rota and then the man snaps his fingers and problem solved."

"That's because he knows what a valued member of the team you are. Your commitment is one of your best qualities. "

"I feel like we should hug or something!"

"Just get going wise guy; you have a few patients to see before you head out."

Nick nodded in agreement, patting Ted on the shoulder as he left to do his final rounds.

As he walked, he checked his notes. He only skimmed the information; he didn't actually need to look at the variety of charts to know his patients. Still, he didn't want to miss anything; his head felt like it was packed with cotton wool - a hangover without the alcohol.

The situation with Laura had gotten under his skin, even though he knew the feelings he had were irrational. He also knew that they were formed in jealousy, because of her growing relationship with Pearson. Nick couldn't even bring himself to say his name; it wouldn't be the first time a man had stolen her heart. He couldn't blame Laura for that, how could he? He had never been able to tell her how he felt. He would follow her to the furthest corners of the planet; he had been doing since they were five years old.

Nick ran a hand through his hair, wondering how he could resolve the situation. He knew he could never grow to like James Pearson. Matt had been different, though he had resented him like hell in the beginning. He knew he had to tell Laura how he felt before it was too late, and he lost her forever. What scared Nick, more than Laura falling in love with another man, was her rejection. He didn't want it to affect their friendship; it had sustained him for more years than he cared to remember, though it was becoming more and more difficult to remain her confidant.

As he reached his destination, Nick pushed these thoughts from his mind; it was time to get back to work. He tucked the files under his arm and forcing a smile, he entered the private room of patient number one.

"What am I, the Laura and Nick counselling service?" Jo asked as she sat across from half of the terrible twosome.

"I'm sorry for putting you in the middle," Nick said, with a small smile. "It's good to see you."

"Oh cut the crap, I'm not away that often. Though granted I wouldn't be here right now if it wasn't for Monica's birthday. As for being in the middle, I always have been when it comes to you and Laura." She paused long enough to take his hand. "I'm worried about you Nicky. You don't have to tell me how you feel about her, because I already know, I've always known. What I can't understand is why you are letting that come between you now."

In truth, he was the first person she called to see upon arriving home. When she landed on his doorstep, Nick had been so pleased to see her that she immediately felt guilty for not coming before. He had always been there for her, and she felt she had let him down a little in the friendship department.

"I just can't deal with it anymore. I think it's because we have been spending so much time together and I dared to let myself hope," Nick said.

"And then James Pearson came on to the scene." Jo concluded.

"Yes, I guess so."

Jo nodded her head in silent understanding. She had meant what she said; she was worried about him. Nick had always possessed such quiet strength, his size and his personality were both a dominating force, but at that moment he seemed like a mere boy. She looked around her, at the uncharacteristic disarray in his living environment.

Although it was far from a stereotypical bachelor pad, Nick had all the gadgets one might expect. In terms of décor, he was a minimalist. The room they were in was painted an off white with only two items of furniture, one of them being a large battered, leather sofa as its centerpiece. Jo knew Nick spent many hours on his trusty old couch, which had been his first purchase after graduating from medical school. She also recalled spending many an evening stretched across the sofa, watching old favourites and sharing popcorn with her two friends.

The only other furniture was a media centre, consisting of all the latest technology, and three bookshelves. These contained a mixture of his favourite volumes and a vast collection of DVDs; clearly Nick was a film buff through and through.

It was, however, quite apparent from the present condition of the space, that Nick was suffering due to recent events in his life. His house was usually spotless, often bordering on sterile in its cleanliness. This, on the other hand, was one of those rare occasions when Jo had seen disorder in his home.

Nick was methodical, though he wouldn't admit it. He did not enjoy chaos in his private space, unless there was a legitimate reason for it. Laura was his complete opposite in that respect. She was a hoarder and her home was full of knick-knacks collected over the years. Jo couldn't help wondering if Nick was, unconsciously, creating an atmosphere that she would be comfortable in, to make himself feel closer to her. Smiling slightly at her amateur psychology, Jo turned her attention back to her friend.

"Why don't you just tell her how you feel?"

"I'm frightened of losing her, and, I know this is going to make me seem like a petulant child, but part of me finds it hard to believe that she doesn't already know. I mean, she must suspect something right? Sometimes I get angry that she's so ignorant about that part of me, but then again she lives in a world of her own most of the time!" Nick said, shaking his head.

"I have to admit that I have often wondered myself. Though in fairness, you've spent years hiding your feelings because of Matt."

"I know." He nodded. "I almost told her once; the night of my graduation, but I bottled out in the end."

Jo raised her eyebrows questioningly. "What made you change your mind?"

"I've never told anyone this before. It's one of those memories I have packed away somewhere in the deep recesses of my mind." As he started to tell Jo about it, the details came flooding back until he felt lost in the memory of it.

The party was in full swing. His graduation had coincided with the purchase of his first flat so he decided to throw a party. Laura had been drinking for most of the day, and she wasn't a drinker, so she was a little worse for wear. To make matters worse, his friends from university had started a drinking game and Lara did not understand the rules, which meant that every time she took her turn it involved a shot of punch. The ingredients were anyone's guess; it was only because she passed out on a bean-bag that Nick realised he had neglected his duties of watching out for her. When Laura finally came to, the party was virtually over. Nick sat with her, remorseful that he had not taken better care of her.

"You looked wonderful on that stage today. You know how proud I am to be your friend don't you? I love ya, you big lug," Laura said, hugging him dramatically.

Laughing, Nick pulled her away from him. "You're really are out of it aren't you? This is the first time I've seen you like this. You're kind of funny when you're less than coherent!"

Laura pulled a face at him and leaned back, struggling to bring him into focus. "Who are you again?" she asked and he roared with laughter.

She looked hurt that he was mocking her, so Nick took her face in his hands. "You are a silly girl, but I love you too!"

When Laura didn't say anything, his heart started to beat faster. He felt an urge to tell her that his feelings for her had grown stronger. With a surge of confidence he lowered his lips to hers and kissed her softly. Laura moaned against his mouth, causing a rush of adrenalin. At the same time he was acutely aware of how drunk she was. He realised that it was not the right time, so he pulled himself away from her.

"Stay where you are, Blue. I'm going to kill this party. It's time to take you home."

Laura was asleep when he returned, so he found a blanket from the cupboard and carried her to the sofa. He covered her gently, thinking that he would tell her in the morning, when she was sober.

In the end Nick didn't get the opportunity, because as soon as Laura was fit enough to communicate with another living person, she didn't stop talking about a man she met at the party. There had been slight hope when she started to remember the kiss, but Nick did not have the nerve to correct her when she presumed it was the man of her affections.

"That man, I presume, was Matt?" Jo asked, bringing her friend back to the present. She could not bear to see the sadness in his face.

"Yes." Nick smiled at the irony of his situation.

"You must have been a little angry with her back then for not knowing it was you?" Jo asked intuitively.

"Not angry, but certainly disappointed. I didn't expect fireworks and violins or any of that slush you women like so much; a memory would have been nice though!"

"I can't believe you've never told me that before."

"I don't suppose it came up. I think this thing with Dad, coupled with her new obsession with the letters, has forced me to see that I can't continue pretending," Nick said.

"Nicky, don't be so hard on yourself. For a start, you weren't pretending to be her friend; you've always been that. Don't beat yourself up for keeping this from her; you have never been anything other than the person she can rely on."

"I know, but even so, it's nice to hear."

"I think it's time to bite the bullet, so to speak, and tell her what you are feeling. Anything has got to be better than this torment of your own making."

Nick picked up a cushion and threw it in her direction. "When did you become so wise?"

"I've always been the brains of the operation!"

He laughed, which was great to hear. It wasn't like him to be so uptight, Nick had a ready laugh, and Jo would never tire of hearing it.

"I'm really glad you came - I know, I know, we have rules - but you are the only one I can talk to about this and it feels good to get it out."

Jo jumped to her feet. "In that case, whilst you are in the mood for sharing, get your old friend a glass of wine and you can tell me all about the mess you've gotten yourself into with the delightful, but misguided Charlie."

The small flashing envelope in Nick's in-box, felt like a salvation; like water after a long draught. He had been waiting to hear from her for days, and now he had finally received a reply, he was almost too frightened to open it. He took a deep breath, and feeling like a third grader, pressed to open the message.

To: Nicholas.Carey@cfw.co.uk
From: lauraBSL@interpreter.co.uk

Dear Nicky

I think the words you were looking for are real hum dinger! And I don't need to see your ugly mush to know how sorry you are ☺

Seriously though, I'm sorry for over-reacting. We definitely need to talk.

I love ya, you big lug

Blue x (literally – I hate it when we fight!)

Nick let out a sigh, the relief washing over him. He had known, deep down, that she would not hold a grudge, but he also knew he was not out of the woods yet. He had made a decision to tell her how he felt. It didn't have to come between them; he had lived with it for years. But now, it was eating him up inside, and he knew that though his life would be nothing without her, the secret would destroy him if he didn't rid himself of it.

There were only four days to Monica's party; Nick didn't want to tell her before then, it wouldn't be fair. He would tell her afterwards; perhaps the following day. He didn't want to leave it too long, because he planned to visit an old friend in London before returning to work; they would both need some space.

He didn't allow himself to think about her response; it was partly a survival instinct. After what happened to his father, he realised that life was too short to be only half of who you are. His job was also important to him, and he didn't want to become so wrapped up in his own drama that it affected the person his patients had come to expect.

Nick tried to quell any negative thoughts; they were not productive. He was glad for the distraction when his mobile chimed. He glanced at the screen and saw that it was Charlie and instantly brightened. Since he had explained the nature of their relationship to Jo, he felt cleansed somehow of any guilt. He owed a lot to Charlie, she was a sweet girl and right now she needed him. When he answered the call, Nick did not have to work at the pleasure in his voice.

Chapter Sixteen

My Dearest Laura

This is the last letter I will be writing to you (you know what I mean!); these communications have served their purpose.

I would like you to continue writing to me in your journal once in a while; I will always watch out for you, but I feel closer to you at those times.

I think, knowing you as I do, that you needed a gentle push from me so that you could move on. Whatever happens next will not affect what we have; that can never die.

I know you probably feel as though I am deserting you again, and I can forgive you in this instance for the 'drama'; I would feel the same. But it will hinder you in the long run, if I continue to take over your life in this way. Be thankful for this time we had, it was a gift. If arms could materialise on the page and take on a life of their own I would hug you, but as that is not possible I have words. So, my darling, know I will always love you and that it means a lot to me that you are happy. You only get one life, so live it.

Until next we meet.

Matt

James stared at the letter, as he toyed with the idea of showing it to Laura. This time when the words had been making their way onto the page he had anticipated every word. It almost felt like Matt was dictating the letter in his head. This experience alone had given him a powerful sense of being a slave to the text. It was not an unusual feeling, nor unwelcome, but he still could not banish the thoughts that he had somehow orchestrated it.

James knew he was over analysing; just reading the letter should be proof enough that he was not the author. It was just so final and if he was honest with himself, unexpected. For selfish reasons he did not want to break the ties he had to Laura; whatever the reason for them. At the same time he knew he should give her the letter.

Having reached a decision, he got out of his car and made his way towards Laura's office. James had called ahead and asked her to lunch; when she suggested meeting at the interpreting service he was unexpectedly touched. It meant that he would potentially meet her colleagues, which meant that she wasn't keeping their growing friendship a secret.

With a now familiar excitement, he entered the building and walked in the direction he was being guided. The signage was very clear; he was so used to walking into buildings that were a maze of misinformation. James was impressed with the design of the interior; the well lit foyer and sheer elegance of his surroundings caught his attention immediately. A passageway led to the interpreting offices, this too was well lit and thankfully did not have the usual ready-made office furniture with compulsory tropical plant. The seating area had a plush leather couch, with a coffee machine that belonged in an industrial kitchen. It made James smile. He had only known Laura a short time, but he knew only too well about her addiction to coffee. This was just her version of an intravenous drip.

He was about to press a buzzer, when the outer office door opened. A tall woman, with red hair she obviously had difficulty taming, came out into the reception area.

"You must be James?" she said, with a husky tone that surprised him.

"I am." James agreed, mesmerised.

"I'm Phoebe, and I'm under strict instructions to entertain you whilst Laura finishes her meeting. She won't be long, come and meet

David," Phoebe said with such a rush of enthusiasm that James could only nod his head.

"David, our guest is here. Don't forget we are on our best behaviour!" She spoke to someone as she opened another door to their left.

James smiled; no wonder Laura loved her job so much.

"Oh course, we can't scare off the civilians!" a young man answered her, already on his feet.

"Hi, I'm David. I'm sure you've heard all about me!" he said to James, winking.

"Come on, you two, the man hasn't even got into the office yet." The voice came from another man at the far end of the room. James guessed it must be Duncan; he was older than David and had a more laid back posture that Laura had described.

"That's all right," James told him. "Laura has told me so much about you, I wouldn't expect anything less."

"Oh, you are divine!" Phoebe breathed from beside him, making James bark with laughter.

"No seriously, I want to marry you and have lots of babies!"

"Perhaps we should get to know each other a little better first!" James grinned, enjoying their playful banter; he felt right at home.

"Just ignore Phoebe; she falls in love every five minutes." David said, backing away as though he expected Phoebe to attack.

"I can't help it if I find so many things attractive in a man. A voice; a pair of hands; a physic; the use of language; sense of humour; intelligence; compassion; smouldering eyes. Imagine if I found all that in one man?" Phoebe motioned for James to take a seat at an empty desk.

"You've been working with Craig again haven't you?" Duncan asked her. "He always puts you in a playful mood".

She was about to respond when an office door opened to James's right and Laura stood at the entrance in mock indignation.

"I can't leave you alone for five minutes, can I? I ask you to go easy on our guest and you hit him with everything you've got!" She turned to James. "I only have myself to blame. If I hadn't said anything they would have been most civilised."

"We were just living up to the interpreters' reputation of being pretentious, conceited, exhibitionists!" David said, making Laura giggle. It was a lovely sound and it made James want to hear it again.

Phoebe turned to him with a serious expression. "We usually let off steam in this way. Some of the stresses of our job have to find an avenue somewhere and Laura wouldn't like you so much if you couldn't be around people who enjoy expressing themselves."

"That's true, Phoebs. I wanted James to see what I see every day when I come to work. I knew if I told you to behave you would do the exact opposite."

"I can see why you love it, working here. Particularly the vat of coffee in the entrance," James replied and they all smiled.

"Speaking of coffee, I think you've had enough of a culture shock for one day. Shall we go?"

"Sure, it was nice to meet you all," James said to the group.

Phoebe winked at him. "The pleasure was all ours!"

Laura grabbed her jacket from the peg and led James out of the office. As he followed her through the main entrance he had the uncanny feeling that her cheerfulness was a cover for how she was really feeling. He seemed to know things when it came to her, and it scared him. It took James a long time to get to know someone; he was naturally intuitive but connecting with people was not a strong suit. He felt as though he had known Laura for most of his life and wondered more than once if these feelings were a residue of some sort, from the letters. To believe that though, he would have to believe in the paranormal and he wasn't ready for that yet.

James followed Laura to a café bar nearby. They didn't speak as they walked, but it was not an awkward silence. He was impressed by the place she had chosen, and suspected that it was one of Laura's favourite cafés. He was slightly overwhelmed by the lunch menu; there was so much to choose from. He settled on coffee to begin with, until he decided which one of the delightful dishes to opt for. Laura didn't seem to mind his indecision; she was quite happy to wait.

"So," she said when they were seated. "What is it that you wanted to talk to me about? I'm guessing you have another letter?"

James didn't answer immediately; his eyes roamed the environment, taking it all in. There were very few people in their section of the cafe, most customers were seated in the dining area, but he was glad they could talk openly. He sank back into the leather chair, and looked across at Laura. The air which escaped from the cushions as they took his weight, sounded like a sigh – it mirrored his own.

"Yes, it's another letter, but I'm not sure you'll like this one," James said. He pushed it across the table, being mindful of the drop of latte the waitress had spilt.

Laura picked the paper up, a frown shadowing her face. She read in silence, her expression unreadable. When she finally looked up there were tears in her eyes. "He's wrong about one thing," she said hoarsely.

James raised his eyebrows in question. He felt like a fraud, especially as he still wasn't convinced that her dead husband was communicating with her.

"It doesn't feel like he is abandoning me because I never really had him this time. I was devastated when he died, but it didn't really feel like abandonment then either."

"You must have felt anger at some point - it is part of the grieving process." James pointed out.

"Oh, don't get me wrong, I was mad at everyone and everything for a while; you could say the whole world. But I never blamed Matt, or at least not consciously."

"I think he probably picked up on your emotions," James told her, and for the first time believed it to be true; that her husband was out there somewhere.

"He knows me well!"

James frowned at the tense she chose to use, as thought Matt was still with her. "I can tell from the intimacy of the letters. Sometimes they felt almost too personal for me to read; even though they were written by my hand."

Laura laughed, nodding her head in understanding. "You should try interpreting a phone call between lovers!" she said.

"What do you mean?"

"I had a deaf client who regularly used the service to contact his hearing fiancée. I had to interpret sweet nothings down the phone, but I don't think either of them had a problem with it. It just felt a little strange, even though I interpreted for my family growing up; intimacy was never something that came up." Laura laughed at the expression on his face. "Thankfully, there is now the internet, so they can communicate directly and not have to rely on a third party."

"That's good," James replied, not really knowing what else to say.

They sat in silence for a few moments, each enjoying their coffee. He was about to ask her more about interpreting for her family when Nick popped into his head and the question escaped him before he could stop it.

"How are things with Nick?"

"You mean after the argument? We haven't actually spoken yet, though we've communicated electronically." Laura looked lost in thought for a moment. "He's been a pillar of support to me since Matt died. There was a time when he phoned me everyday, just to check in."

"It sounds like you have a special bond," James said, smiling at her.

"You could say that. I have another friend, Jo. When we were in college, the three of us were inseparable."

"It…" James was interrupted by a chirping sound from the pager on his belt. His eyes lit up when he heard it, a grin spreading across his face. "That will be Danielle, my sister. Unless it's another false alarm, that sound means my niece or nephew are on their way."

"That's wonderful!"

"I'm sorry to cut our lunch short, but I'd better get to the hospital. I'm the standby birthing partner," James said.

"Of course, I completely understand."

As they finished their drinks, James promised he would call Laura when he had news. He was excited about being involved in the birth, but at the same time he knew how disappointed his brother-in-law, George, would be. George worked on oil rigs, and had done for almost four years. It wasn't a job he particularly enjoyed; he saw it as an investment for their future. Ironically, this was his final job; he was due home in three days.

James walked Laura back to the office and high tailed it over to the hospital, he was oddly nervous about becoming an uncle for the first time, but he intended to remember every detail so he could tell George about it.

James rushed into his sister's hospital room. His jaw nearly hit the ground when he saw the baby in her arms. He had been thirty five minutes at the outside, and had been expecting a long labour based on the nightmares she had been having for months.

"Hi, Uncle James!" Danielle whispered, sounding tired but elated.

"How did this happen?" he asked, moving closer to the bed.

Danielle laughed. "I think you're a little old to be asking questions about the birds and the bees; were you really expecting a delivery from the stork?"

James looked at her; he didn't have to say anything because she knew what he was thinking.

"Come on, Eric is waiting," she said. "I will tell you all about it."

James took his nephew in his arms and felt an overwhelming sense of pride. "Hi there, little man." He stared into an unblinking set of blue eyes. "I thought newborns were supposed to sleep?" he asked.

"I'm sure he will, but right now he wants to take a good look at his surroundings and he probably hasn't recovered from his trip down the birth canal!"

"Gross," James said, pretending to cover Eric's ears. "He's beautiful sis, we are truly blessed."

Danielle told him about the speed of her delivery, explaining that she had been in labour for a while without even realising it. James didn't let go of his nephew until he absolutely had to, the fact that he was using his new lungs with vigour indicated that he wasn't happy. It turned out he was hungry; having finished his observations of this strange new world.

As his sister fed Eric he flicked through a magazine at the side of the bed. He was enjoying the time with his family, and felt truly happy, until a young nurse came into check on Danielle. As she got closer to the bed the atmosphere changed dramatically, and James was filled with a deep sadness; bordering on despair. It took him by surprise, and for a moment he was paralysed by it. When he regained his composure, all he wanted to do was put his arms around the nurse and promise it would be all right. He was so disturbed by these feelings that he crossed to the other side of the room to distance himself.

"She had a miscarriage six months ago and just found out she can't have any more children," Danielle said, when the nurse had gone.

"So why is she working on a maternity ward?" James asked. He did not question how she knew he felt something when the nurse was in the room.

"I don't know. I don't even know why she told me, it was just one of those moments when we bonded and she needed to share her anguish with someone."

"She still does." James observed, not meeting his sister's eyes.

"Are we going to talk about this? Your feelings have returned since the letters haven't they?" Danielle asked.

"Maybe later. Right now, I am going to go out and buy my nephew a filthy amount of toys and fill the house with them."

"The doctor said I can go home tomorrow, if I hear any more I'll let you know."

"Thanks, I'll see you soon." James kissed them both on the head, and left the room. He didn't have anywhere to go in such a hurry; he just needed to think about what had just happened.

Chapter Seventeen

```
From: Dani
```
Bro... the doctor told me I can leave first thing in the morning... so if you could bring the things I mentioned... that would be great. George is on his way home - should see his boy by tomorrow night...can't wait... sis xx

"Here's to Eric," Barry said, raising his glass for perhaps the seventh time.

"I think you're only supposed to wet the baby's head once." James pointed out, though he held up his glass too.

"If the birth of a baby isn't cause for celebration then I don't know what is."

James scoffed. "You'd find an excuse to celebrate posting a letter."

"Well someone has to appreciate the postal service. Here's to *Royal Mail*!" Barry joked, touching the rim of his glass with the one James was holding. "Seriously though, buddy. I'm just trying to show you that we have cause for celebration. You don't seem to know that at the moment."

"I appreciate it. You're a good friend."

"Don't forget it." Barry agreed. "Here's to friendship."

James raised his glass higher this time, smiling at him.

"I'm serious, James - If you want to talk about it."

"It's been an unusual couple of weeks, that's all. When I figure it out, I'll share it with you," James said.

"Fair enough."

He didn't know what to say to that. He really wanted to share his news with Barry, but he was afraid of what his friend would make of it. He was saved by the bell, or in his case, by a pal. With his usual sense of timing, Tony sauntered into the bar, just as the atmosphere was getting a little awkward.

"Who died?" Tony asked, patting James on the back.

Barry jumped down from his stool, and moved to hug their friend. "Oh, Tony, mate… thank God the rumour isn't true."

"Very funny," Tony remarked, pushing him away. "You both obviously need a few lessons in the art of having a good time."

"We were waiting for you," Barry said, moving to order a fresh round of drinks.

"Did you catch the news?" Tony asked.

James looked at him suspiciously; it was something they asked one another – they usually covered the news. "Is this going to be another of your sick jokes?"

"No, I'm serious. It's all over local and national radio. I'm surprised you haven't been summoned to the scene, Barry."

"Spit it out, Tone!" James said.

"A young nurse is on top of the general infirmary, threatening to jump."

"You were sitting on a scoop like that and you came here?" Barry asked, shaking his head.

"Hey, it's not my bag, besides there are photographers and cameramen a plenty." Tony defended himself.

"I'd better make a few calls," Barry murmured. He wandered off to find a better signal on his phone.

"Hey, it's not like the prime minister got shot or something, there will be other stories," Tony said to James, mistaking his look of horror for guilt.

"It's not the story, I have a feeling I know the woman. Does she work on a maternity ward by any chance?"

"Yes, how did you know?"

"Lucky guess. Listen, tell Barry I had to run, I have something to take care of," James said, feeling like he had taken a blow to the stomach.

"Like hell, you've been drinking. I'll take you down there, and we'll grab Baz on the way," Tony replied. He had made the decision and had no intention of backing down, James didn't even try. If he hadn't been in shock he would have laughed at the expression on Barry's face when Tony practically picked him up and deposited him at the car.

On the journey to the infirmary, James was vaguely aware of Barry screeching instructions into his mobile phone. He had no idea why he needed to get to the hospital so badly, all he knew was that it couldn't happen to him a second time. Getting anywhere near the hospital would take a miracle, roads had been blocked in the centre; police had the whole area cordoned off. When Tony parked the car, as near as he could, James jumped out. "Listen, guys, I don't really have time to explain right now, but I know this woman. I need to …" James was rudely interrupted by his mobile phone. He was going to ignore it, until he noticed it was his sister.

"Hi, Dan, what's going on?" he asked.

"They managed to get her inside. The crisis team are probably around here somewhere," Danielle told him. "I couldn't ring you before I knew she was safe."

"Thanks, honey. I will come by in the morning, we can talk then."

James was consciously aware that his two friends were staring at him with interest. It seemed that he had over-reacted; he felt foolish for rushing to the scene like some would-be super hero.

"She's not going to jump," he said, not knowing what else to say.

Barry had the same problem. "Crisis over then."

"Not for that poor girl. Do you know her well?" Tony asked.

"My sister Danielle has seen more of her," James replied, evading the question without having to lie.

"What do you say we all hit my pad with a pizza, and a few beers?" Barry asked. "You can tell us all about this mystery woman."

"Good idea." Tony clapped his hands together. "Let's rock."

James didn't have the heart to say no. He wasn't ready to have that discussion, but he didn't relish the thought of being alone either. Instead, James nodded his agreement and began working on diversion tactics.

It was a little after midnight, and James knew if he didn't leave Barry's house soon, the conversation he had been avoiding for hours would spill out of him like a dirty secret. Tony had left a few minutes before, making a parting joke about being under the thumb. They all knew that Tony, though a kind soul, was nobody's fool and certainly not a push over.

James knew it was time to go, he just didn't like the idea of moving. He was comfortable where he was, sat on a huge bean bag that defied anyone to move, as soon as they sunk into its depths. Barry's house was under renovation. He wasn't the type of person to tackle the job one room at a time, so he started on a section of each room of the house; to anyone else it was chaos. Barry moved most of the furniture out of his lounge. The only things remaining were a wall mounted plasma TV and three bean bags for his visitors.

"Don't tell me… you have to go?" Barry said, as James won his battle with the bean bag.

"Yeah, I told Danielle I would be at the hospital early, and she wants me to pick up a few things."

"Are you ever going to tell me what's bothering you, or are we going to pretend your behaviour tonight was not out of the ordinary?"

"Can you pretend?" James asked, knowing Barry would not accept his attempts at aversion any longer. When his friend said nothing, James sank back into the comfortable material of his seat, finally giving in. "You're going to think I need to be sectioned when you hear this," he said, without humour.

"Too late, I know you need professional help, so just spill."

James told him about meeting Laura, about the letters and about his feelings when he had been around the nurse. Barry listened patiently, not interrupting, or questioning his explanations.

"That explains the dreams anyway," Barry said when James reached the end. It was so completely not what James had expected to hear that at first he thought the alcohol had clouded his brain.

"Have you ever wondered why we are drawn to certain people?" Barry smiled. "How we seem to connect with them without knowing why?"

"You've lost me," James said, thinking he had better lay off the alcohol.

"I'm just saying that we are more alike than you think. We both use humour as a defence mechanism, we both work in a field we were drawn to because we can read people."

"All right, I'll give you that. But where do dreams come into it?"

"Oh. I suppose that's just my way of working things out in my head."

"Whilst you sleep?"

"Yes. My dreams tend to contain messages that help me in some way; they are usually hard to decipher, and it takes a while." Barry waited for James to say something, when he didn't, he continued. "When I met you James, I knew that you used more than a gut feeling to know the things you know about people. I used to think you were exceptionally good at reading between the lines, but whether you know it or not, you pick up facts without a person having to open their mouths."

"There are many people who have a gift for doing that," James pointed out.

"And the emotions?"

"That too, but I will accept it's unusual to pick up an emotion from someone without engaging with them, verbally or otherwise."

"It's harder still to respond to letters you've never even seen, based on a few hunches."

James felt like his friend had been abducted by aliens, and someone else had been put in his place.

Barry laughed self consciously. "I'm not saying all this to freak you out. I haven't changed over night - I'm still the person you know. I'm just choosing to share a different part of myself. You'll be pleased to know that I'm sitting on a number of jokes."

"Do you have any theories to share about why this is happening?" James asked.

"Not a clue. I can help you with a little research. I get the impression that the young nurse is just the beginning. I'm happy to be your sounding board."

James let out a sigh, feeling like he was stuck in a dream himself. "I don't suppose the spare room has a roof yet?" he asked.

"Yes, as a matter of fact it does. It's the only room in the house that's finished - mainly because my mom is flying out to visit. Why, do you want to crash?"

"Yeah, I'm worn out." James tried to stand up but the bean bag was fighting back this time.

"No problem, you can crash here any time. Just one thing though…"

"Oh god, you're not going to tell me you see dead people are you?" James said, pulling a face.

"Very funny. I wanted to say that you shouldn't deny who you are, and if there is a part of yourself that you don't understand, you need to create an explanation you can live with."

"Anything you say *Jeremy Kyle!*"

"I'm not myself; someone has taken over my ability to think and is putting words into my mouth!" Barry shot back.

"Eat shit!"

"Goodnight to you too my friend."

James didn't reply; he gave a mock salute and turned towards the stairs. This had definitely been a day for the books, he couldn't write this stuff; maybe he should try.

Chapter Eighteen

Dear Matt

I want to thank you, or the powers that be, for making our recent correspondence possible. I've said it before, but I never dreamt that you would find a way to reply.

I know now, that you will always look out for me and I'm grateful for that too. This is not the last entry I will write, but I don't need to do it as often. It's funny because this whole thing is probably something you and I would talk about. Phoebe did a little research and there is something called automatic writing; I don't think James is ready to accept that theory yet.

Anyway, I have a mountain of work to do. Remember that you will always be in my thoughts and my heart, no matter what.

All my love,
Laura x

Laura shut down her computer, relieved that she had managed to battle her way through 63 emails. She looked at the clock, sighing heavily; it was 1am and she should be catching up on her sleep. There was only one problem - her frequent insomnia was back, which meant there was no point going to bed until she could first find a way to wind down.

She padded to the kitchen, touching the coffee percolator as she passed; it was cold. She switched on the kettle, settling for instant. As she prepared her cup, she wondered what she could do to kill the time. The flat was spotlessly clean, and she had watched her favourite movies twice already. Her mind was far too active for her to do nothing at all. Laura stirred the water in her cup absently, she didn't feel like reading, and she had already written in her journal, so there was nothing left to do but channel hop.

As she was carrying her drink into the living room, her mobile phone cut through the silence, making her jump. Laura glanced at the display from where it sat on the coffee table; she was surprised to see that James was ringing so late. Out of curiosity she pressed the receive button, accepting his call.

"Hi, James," she said softly into the receiver, as though trying not to wake an imaginary guest.

"Laura, sorry to ring so late but I just got your email and as we both suffer sleepless nights from time to time, I thought I would give it a shot."

Laura smiled, he sounded as exhausted as she felt. They had both grown tired of their restlessness; it felt good that someone knew how she was feeling.

"Don't worry. I only had an hour or two with Paramount planned," she told him taking a seat.

"My thoughts are driving me to drink, literally, so I needed a friendly voice."

"Do you fancy sharing them with me?" she asked him, wondering where he was.

"I was hoping you'd be more of a distraction. Tell me your news; we haven't caught up in a few days."

"Let me see. Oh yes, Jane brought her baby daughter in to see us today. She is beautiful, and a delight for her new parents. We didn't get anything productive done for the rest of the day, but that's not important," Laura told him, between sips of coffee.

"Sounds like fun. I can just imagine how everything stopped with a baby in your midst. My nephew has already taken over the Jackson household."

"Of course, how is Eric?"

"He's adorable. I can't believe how tiny and vulnerable he is. I feel so humbled in his presence," James said. Laura could almost hear the shake of his head.

"Eric is lucky to have an uncle who loves him so much." Laura was starting to feel sleepy, lulled by the sound of his voice. She sank deeper into the cushions. "Hey, if I fall asleep during our conversation, you won't be offended will you?" she asked.

"Not at all, but make sure you're sitting down. I don't want to hear a crash when you literally 'fall asleep!'"

Laura laughed "You have a soothing voice; you could be a late night DJ. I'd never have problems sleeping then."

"Gee, thanks. That was a nice way of telling me I can send a group of people to sleep with my dulcet tones."

"You know what I mean. I just have this thing about voices. There was a TV programme years ago, I think it was called *'Beauty and the Beast;'* a series based loosely on the Disney concept. The 'beast' was called Vincent and he had the most incredible voice," Laura tried to explain.

"That went over my head on so many levels!"

She grinned, enjoying his sense of humour. "All right, so I tend to babble. I should have stopped at 'you have a soothing voice."

"I'll take that," James replied; she could tell he was smiling too.

"What kind of day did you have?" Laura asked him.

"A strange one - the reason for my insomnia I'm sure."

"Are you ready to talk about it yet?"

"Well if truth be told, you may be the best person to talk to. My family are too close, most of my friends would never understand, and one of them is part of the problem," he said.

"Talk about cryptic, do I have to guess?"

James laughed, some of the tension leaving his voice. "The letters, although new, are not the first strange thing to happen to me." He paused, but Laura did not interrupt him. "When I was a boy, my mother used to tell me I was gifted with a strong intuition and that it made me special. I hated it, I didn't like anything I couldn't explain and I guess it turned into fear. I could pick up on other people's emotions and I didn't like it, so I started to avoid group situations."

When there was another silence, Laura waited patiently, before she realised he needed a little prompting. "Is that why you were a loner?" she asked, remembering a previous conversation.

"In part, yes, I suppose that had something to do with it. It is also a part of who I am. I was happy discovering new worlds between the pages of my books, or creating my own through writing. My characters were my friends, and my family have always given me what I need."

"So you distanced yourself from people?"

"Most of the time. There was one incident in college that affected me pretty badly. Only my family know about it, but I guess you need to understand before I tell you the rest."

Laura listened as he told her about a tragedy that struck someone he knew. A boy he shared most of his classes with, and whom he had started to become close to, had taken his own life.

"I used to sense how sad he was inside, it wasn't anything he did, or said; I felt physically affected just being with him. When I tried to bring it up, he dismissed it; he wouldn't admit to a problem. Then one day I had a dream. It was a strange dream because, in it, I was Jake, and I was flying. I felt happy and at peace. It sounds strange but I felt no fear, and because of the nature of how I was, or rather he was, experiencing flight - there was no fear in that either. Like it was completely natural. When I woke up, I knew something was wrong and I couldn't shake it. I later found out that Jake had jumped from a block of high rise flats and plummeted to his death."

Laura gasped, her heart going out to both the young man who had been tortured enough to take his own life, and the man who was still tormented by it.

"After that I went off the rails a little. I didn't like to get too close to people and I denied a big part of myself. I pushed it out of the way so I didn't have to think about what it all meant."

"What do you think now?" she asked, suspecting he had analysed the experience from all possible angles.

"I just don't know, Laura. I do believe we all have an energy that some people are more sensitive to than others, even when a person is no longer living. Whether that is an advanced part of our senses I just don't know; the more I think about it, the more confused I get."

Laura looked at the clock above her television, it was almost 2 am. She was now fully awake, and knew there was no chance of sleep. "Hey, do you fancy continuing this discussion over coffee?" she asked him.

"Sure, what did you have in mind?"

"Well, there is a 24-hour superstore on Gladstone Boulevard, I'm sure we will grab something wet and warm there."

"Yes, I know it. I can be there in about twenty minutes."

"Great, then I will see you in 20!"

The store was only a few minutes away from her apartment, so Laura was early. She decided to have a coffee whilst she waited and persuaded the waitress to bring another drink over when James arrived.

Laura watched the entrance to the café thoughtfully. She was not usually impulsive and it felt good to be taking control. When James came into her line of vision she was shocked at how tired he looked. She rose to her feet and walked to meet him, hugging him wordlessly when he stood in front of her with a weary smile. James hugged her back, murmuring thanks under his breath because she had understood he needed it.

He grinned when the waitress arrived with more coffee. ""Are you a regular here?" he asked.

"This is the first time I've been here in over a year, believe it or not. Waitresses just tend to sense how desperate I am for coffee; it is the delirium in my eyes!"

"Or waiters," James added, pulling a face that reminded her of Nick.

"Yes, anyone who happens to serve me coffee. But you were telling me why you can't get to sleep at night."

"Yes, I wasn't doing a very good job of it either," James replied between sips of coffee.

"I wouldn't say that. You just started where any good story starts; at the beginning."

"I suppose so. It's strange, for years nothing much happened apart from a few hunches that were of no real significance, and then I met you."

Laura smiled, she had often marvelled at the circumstances herself.

"When I first realised the letters were connected to you, I thought I had orchestrated them just so that I could meet you again. I felt such a strong connection to you during our first meeting that I was taken in by it. We've talked about this before, but I never really told you my theory about the emotional attachment I felt."

"Sounds intriguing." Laura prompted.

"Well, like I said, I sense strong emotional energy, for want of a better word, from people I come into contact with. I haven't experienced the strength of feeling I got around you in a long time, so I was confused by it at first. I now realise I was picking up residual energy; perhaps your love for your husband, or more likely his love for you." James felt liberated for actually saying it out loud.

"I'm not sure how to take that!" Laura smiled at him.

"Oh, don't get me wrong - I was attracted to you, and not only physically. I think two people can be drawn to one another for a number of reasons, and my life is all the better for meeting you."

"That's a lovely thing to say," Laura told him, a little taken aback by his directness.

James laughed self consciously. "I have a reputation for being blunt, but I rarely open up in this way on a personal level. Now I seem to be doing it all the time. One of my closest friends, who I didn't think had a serious bone in his body, suddenly turned into an expert in psychology!"

"Is that the friend you hinted at earlier?" Laura asked.

"One and the same. But before I tell you about Barry, I want to tell you about Sonia. I met her on the maternity ward when I was visiting

Danielle. Just being around her was difficult; I picked up such powerful emotions that I almost bolted for the exit. Dani told me she had a miscarriage recently, which left her unable to have children. I now know that the sadness I felt came from deep within her." James paused for a moment when the waitress came with a re-fill. "I was haunted by her; it felt like history was repeating itself."

"What did you do?"

"I spoke to Danielle, told her all about the things I picked up. Luckily, based on our conversation, Danielle was able to reach her when she hit rock bottom. She is a very talented lady, my sister; Sonia couldn't have gotten anyone better."

"That's incredible!"

"I know. It makes my head spin just thinking about it. Then, Barry turns into Mr. Sensitive, which completely blows my mind."

"The friend, right?"

"Right. When I told him about you, and about Sonia, I expected him to freak out or something, but he seemed unsurprised by it."

"And that's a bad thing?" Laura asked, smiling at his reaction.

"It's not a bad thing, but I can't pretend I'm not surprised. I suppose when he mentioned that he has dreams…"

"You're making that up," Laura interjected, suddenly wide awake with interest.

"I couldn't make that up!" James protested. "Since then, Barry has been his usual self, slipping in subtle jokes to goad me."

"What about the dreams?"

"He only told me that the dreams are a way for his subconscious to piece things together."

"I thought that's what most dreams are anyway?" Laura was a little lost.

"Yes, so they say. But I think he picks things up, without even realising it. We both have a habit of doing that. For example, I know the waitress was in a rush to get to work because her name tag is not in the exact place she usually wears it…there are holes worn into the fabric towards the left hand side. I presume she takes here badge off to wash the uniform and the marks indicate she usually wears the tag in the same place."

"How do you know it wasn't like that yesterday?"

"I don't, but working in a café, she probably washes her uniform daily. Another thing I noticed is that she recently held a baby, because of the telltale little white patch on her right shoulder."

"Wow, all that from a few glances."

"Yes, but that's not the only thing. I didn't say the baby was hers, not because I'm afraid of making an assumption, but because I know without a shadow of a doubt that she isn't the mother. I am naturally observant, and pick those things up, but it is the things I know that I cannot explain that scare me. Barry, I presume goes through a similar process in his sleep; everything he sees, everything he picks up from a person, he pieces together in his dreams."

"Oh," Laura said, nodding her head.

"You sound disappointed."

"No. I just thought you were going to tell me he has these dreams in order to help people."

"It sounds like you've been watching too much TV." James joked.

"It could happen. I know you won't believe it, but you've helped me. I don't know the reason we were brought together, but I feel like a weight has been lifted."

"Well, I'm glad. Perhaps now you and Nick can be together." James threw in.

Laura almost choked on her coffee. "Me and Nick?"

"Yes, maybe you are ready for a relationship with someone else now."

"Nick and I are friends. I don't know what made you think…"

"He has a major crush on you," James said simply.

"Nick does not have a crush on me! I think you've had enough coffee mister; you obviously can't keep up with a seasoned drinker."

"Why are you evading the subject?" James asked.

"I'm not evading the subject. Nick and I have been friends forever."

"Maybe so, but that doesn't mean you can't be more."

"Is this because of our little scene in the restaurant?" Laura asked. She was amused by his observation.

"I didn't mean to overstep the mark, forget I said anything."

"That's all right. It's an honest mistake."

James studied her for a moment. He looked like he wanted to say more, but he didn't. Laura felt a little uncomfortable, as though she was being scrutinised. "I suppose I should get back and grab an hour before the sun comes up," she said.

"Of course. Thanks for the chat. I really needed it."

"Anytime."

Laura drained the rest of her coffee, thinking about what he had said. She was convinced James had misread the signals, but something about their conversation made her feel uneasy and she couldn't think why.

Laura's head pounded; it felt like her brain had decided enough was enough and was banging its way out. She had been interpreting for two and a half hours and knew she had to stop soon; she was barely coherent. What should have been a simple team briefing had turned into a nightmare. The department was about to become extinct and emotions were running high. For the deaf professional she had been called to interpret for, it felt like the end of his career. It was the first time her service had accepted a booking from the firm, and it was common practice to ask details of an assignment, so that Rebecca could determine if one or two interpreters were needed. Anything over two hours required a co-worker, but this had supposedly been a twenty minute job. Laura had fallen into that trap many times before; she usually coped with a meeting for up to three hours, but this time she would be lucky if she crawled out of the room.

She informed the employee of her intentions in sign language first, and then announced to the chair of the group that she needed a break. No-one was particularly happy about it, but her tone had not offered them a choice. She waited until someone had done the decent thing and brought her a cup of coffee before wandering outside for some fresh air.

As she sipped the coffee, she closed her eyes, hoping the headache would subside before she went back in. It was anyone's guess how long the meeting would last; she would have to call in the reinforcements eventually.

Laura unclipped the clasp on her bag and rummaged for her emergency medical kit; an interpreter's best friend. Laura had everything in there, for all kinds of emergencies and the headache pills were right on top of the pile. She sighed in frustration when her hand did not immediately find what she was seeking. Laura put her coffee on a window ledge and opened the bag wider. As she did so, she noticed that her mobile was ringing. The display flashed in silent alarm; a slight vibration ran through her hand as she turned it over. When she noticed it was Nick she snatched it up and pressed to accept the call.

"What's up doc?"

"That's still going to be lame, no matter how many times you say it!" Nick said at the other end of the air waves.

"Oh come on now, inside you are laughing."

"Blue, it stopped being cute when we were twelve and I went through my life saving phase."

"It's good to hear from you. I'm hauled up in the meeting from hell - I have a *Night at the Proms* competing for attention in my head!" Laura told him. Nick laughed; a sound she hadn't heard too often lately.

"I missed you," he said simply and it made Laura smile.

"I missed you too."

"Anyway, enough of the mushy stuff; I don't want to hold you up. If I know you, you have a coffee in one hand and two paracetomol in the other," Nick said, and this time it was Laura's turn to laugh.

"Close enough!"

"I just called to see Monica because I wanted to make sure I gave her the present I've been squirreling for; just in case I can't make the party tomorrow night."

"Why, what happened?"

"Nothing happened specifically. I've just been given time off for good behaviour and I'm going to London to visit Dave," Nick said.

"But you can't miss the party!"

"I wouldn't under normal circumstances; I just need to get away right now," Nick explained.

"It won't be the same without you." Laura was disappointed, but he was due for a break.

"Come on, Blue, don't sulk. I know I haven't been the best of friends lately, but I'll do better."

Laura couldn't make him feel bad, even though she had been looking forward to seeing him so she could make things right between them. "I understand that you need to get away," she said.

"Thanks."

"Don't mention it. Call me later, okay, I have to go."

"All right, bye."

"Asta la vista!" Laura said in her worst '*Schwarzenegger*' voice and snapped the phone shut.

She retrieved her cup from the windowsill and hurried back inside. As she put the phone into her bag, her hand touched the emergency kit. Laura closed her eyes, sighing in relief. She pulled out the tables, whilst hurrying down the corridor. When she arrived back at the meeting room, she hesitated long enough to slug down her cold coffee with two painkillers.

Chapter Nineteen

From: Nicky
I will be there in a couple of hours. I have a surprise for you that will bump me up in the popularity stakes! See you soon. Doc x

Laura checked her appearance in the full length mirror. She had hired the gown because none of her clothes seemed to fit her; she had a habit of comfort eating. The dress was a deep red with black chiffon. Laura suspected that the hoop would eventually drive her mad; it had already started to itch. She studied the gloves, trying to decide if they were over the top. The mask that came with the ball gown was made from beautiful rich velvet, matching the colours of the outfit. When she held it to her face she almost laughed; she didn't recognise the women staring back at her and it was a feeling she enjoyed. Her hair helped to create the illusion; usually long and straight, it was now piled on top of her head and soft curls framed her face.

She removed the gloves and threw them on her dresser; deciding they were too much after all. Laura knew exactly what her outfit needed; her grandmother's locket was perfect. She went to the huge walk-in wardrobe that dominated her bedroom and located her jewelry box. It contained her best pieces so it was hidden at the back. As she moved away to turn out the light, a box fell on to the floor from the top shelf. It made her start in alarm because she had been nowhere near it. Puzzled, she looked down and then back up at the shelf. There were several boxes up there; they contained memory albums, keepsakes and old journals, so it was possible that the box now on the floor had worked its way loose.

Laura picked it up thoughtfully, shocked at the amount of dust. It was something she hadn't looked at for quite some time. She lifted the lid, and realised it was the box she kept her graduation certificate inside, as well as other educational information that her parents kept over the years. Laura glanced at the clock, wondering if she had enough time to take a brief trip down memory lane. She didn't know why it was so important; it just felt like the right thing to do. She had twenty minutes before it was time to leave for the party, so that left plenty of time for coffee and a delve in to her younger years.

She sat at the kitchen table, thankful she had taken the gloves off; there was dust everywhere. The first file she pulled out was created by her mother as a graduation gift. It included her best work from nursery to university. Laura sipped her coffee and flicked through the pages. Her attention rested on her English Literature project from High School.

My Soul Mate

There are different kinds of soul mates. My sister, Samantha, for example, is one of my soul mates. She knows what I am thinking without me having to say anything. Sam makes me laugh like no other person does; she makes me see things from another perspective.

Jo is my best friend and we will never be far apart. I know this to be true because we are connected by heart.

My parents are part of me and we have a bond that is near unbreakable; a connection that goes beyond blood.

So, as you can see, this project to define my soul mate is not an easy task. You will be familiar with the term 'like two peas in a pod' which is usually used to describe siblings. In my case, it is how people describe the relationship I share with my friend Nick. It would feel like I had lost a limb if I lost him, something I don't like to think about.

I understand that most definitions of the term soul mate pertain to that of an ideal partner. The idea of writing a list of the characteristics that would be a *'best fit'* are extremely difficult. We all dream of meeting someone we can share ourselves with, and I am one of the worlds romantics.

I have been thinking about this project for some time and I suppose, if I were to follow the text book definition, this person would have similar strengths to the people who make me who I am. What I am trying to say, is that a soul mate should go beyond the surface requirements, if people were able to choose. Though I, like anybody else, could name a few ideals or preferences. I could make a list for example; dark hair, dark eyes, tall and strong, big hands with long fingers, big smile, that kind of thing. But I guess what I really want is what I have with so many people, someone to make me laugh; someone who knows everything about me and likes me anyway; someone who accepts me at my worst and at my best.

In the simplest terms and for the purpose of this assignment my soul mate and I would fit like two halves of a whole; forever connected; two spirits as one. Is that over the top? Expecting too much? Who knows – love comes in many guises and I am open to them all.

Laura stopped reading and chuckled to herself. She had so many romantic ideals; it was just like her to over dramatise a subject. She continued flicking through, until she reached the end of the book. Instead of starting a new one, she left everything as it was so that she could continue reminiscing after the party.

The doorbell made Laura jump, even though she had been expecting it. Nick had telephoned that morning and announced that he would pick her up at 7 o'clock to escort her to the party. She rushed to the door, throwing it open with gusto; she had missed her friend and was thrilled he could make it after all. The sight of Nick in his outfit stopped her in his tracks. In certain situations, he had the power to do that to her, and he had never looked so distinguished; Laura couldn't help but let out a low whistle.

"Mr. Carey, I had forgotten how well you scrub up," she said, hugging him with affection.

"Thanks. I think!"

"Seriously, Nick, you look amazing. That mask is wicked." Laura bubbled. "I am so excited."

"It's an improvement on scrumptious I suppose!"

"Not that again. Come on, let's go, before I turn into a pumpkin, or you do, or I break my slipper…however that goes." Laura grabbed her keys from the dresser. "You haven't said anything about my outfit," she added as they walked down the stairs on the way out.

"You'll pass," Nick said, stepping sideways in anticipation of her jibe.

"No wonder you have such a terrible track record with women," Laura replied, with mock indignation.

"I think the car will make up for it." As if on cue, Laura opened the outer door and saw the white limousine parked in the visitor's spot.

"That is our ride?" she asked incredulously.

"I told you I was going to make it up to you, so I'm escorting you in style."

Laura reached up and gave him a quick kiss on the cheek. She ran forward excitedly to take a better look at their chariot for the evening. "Doc, I love it. I feel like I'm going to the prom!"

"Don't you mean ball? A minute ago you were professing to be *Cinderella*." Nick opened the door for her.

Laura ignored his comment and jumped in. This was her first time in a limousine; she had always wanted to travel in style. She drank in the long, plush, leather seats; savouring everything. Along one side of the limousine there was a bar; set up with optics full of liquor; the lights and glitz that were part of the set up made Laura feel like she was in Vegas. Like a kid in a sweet shop, she began pressing buttons; one of which she discovered, lowered the partition between herself and the driver. Laura laughed softly and pulled Nick into the car; the space reduced immediately when his large frame settled into one of the seats.

"This is like a treasure trove. I will be finding things in here for days."

"I thought you might like it. I really pushed the boat out and ordered champagne too," Nick told her, taking the bottle out of an ice bucket she hadn't even noticed.

"Not that a girl likes to complain, but all this really isn't necessary, Nicky."

"I know, I just wanted to. Besides we are spending the evening at a castle, what could be more fitting than that?"

Laura accepted the glass of champagne from him and took a sip. The bubbles tickled her nose, making her giggle at the sensation. "Wait until you see the castle; it is magnificent - especially at night. The last time I was there, I interpreted for a function. It really was great fun."

"It isn't the place I'm worried about, it's that sister of yours and what she has in store for us." Nick shook his head, knowing that any party organised by a Kane could spell disaster.

Laura thought of her younger sister and marveled at the fact that tonight they would be celebrating her eighteenth birthday. It felt like only yesterday that her parents had passed her to Laura on a cushion. Monica was born prematurely, and had spent several weeks in the hospital before she was allowed home. Laura remembered the ward that had cared for her sister. The child orientated environment was decorated with every popular cartoon character of the time; the primary colours lifted your spirits as you roamed the corridors of the homely ward. In Monica's room, dolphin and other calming sounds were played constantly. Some of them replicating what her sister experienced in the womb. She was so tiny, so delicate lying in her incubation bed, that every protective instinct in Laura had kicked in from the moment she saw her.

Nick had been in awe. It was the first time he seriously thought about becoming a doctor. He would sit in the pediatrics unit for hours, listening to the doctors' and dreaming of one day living their lives. It was around the same time that a baby on the special care unit needed an operation to repair a valve in her heart. She was only seven weeks old, and Nick followed her case with all the fervor of a passionate fifteen year old. Perhaps the doctors had sensed a budding surgeon in their midst because they were very accommodating. Laura remembered one evening in particular, a few weeks after Monica was allowed home, when he declared he was going to become a vascular surgeon. He was so serious, so determined, that she believed him. Laura was proud that he had achieved his dreams. He had the heart of a lion and his patients' lives were blessed when in his care.

When the limousine slowed to a stop, Laura realised that she had been so lost in her thoughts she had missed the journey. She regretted not taking more time to look around; her friend had gone to a lot of trouble.

Nick jumped out first and held the door open for her. He offered his hand to guide her out of the car and for a split second Laura remembered him doing the same thing on her wedding day. Their eyes met for a moment, she didn't have to say anything; Nick knew what she was thinking.

The castle was breathtaking, lit up before them like a fairy tale. She linked her arm through Nick's, and pulled him forward, anxious to join the party. At the courtyard entrance, Laura paused and looked at him.

"Before we go in, I just wanted to say thank you for doing this for me. We both know what a drama queen I can be, but tonight I feel like a princess."

"You are welcome," Nick said smiling "I did it…"

"Hey, Carey, how come she gets a limousine?" Jo said from behind them.

"If you're good, I may let you take a ride in it later," he said.

They hugged each other; it was the first time the three of them had been together in months.

"What are we stood here for? My delightful husband is just parking the car, so I agreed to get the drinks in," Jo said, exchanging a glance with Nick.

"In that case, I'll have a vodka martini!" Laura said, linking her other arm through Jo's.

"Hang on," Nick said. "If we are going to make a grand entrance, I want to be in the middle. I will be the envy of every man in the room with you two on my arm."

"I knew there was a reason we liked him!" Jo smiled, laying her head on his shoulder and fluttering her eyelashes.

"You can quit that, you're still buying the drinks," Nick challenged. Jo laughed in delight, moving forward in time with her friends as they entered the castle. For a moment they were all shocked into silence; they had obviously chosen the wrong entrance because they were plunged into semi darkness as soon as the door closed behind them.

"Want to chance it and go this way, or find the other door?" Laura whispered; her arm tightening around Nick's. He chuckled and squeezed back, taking a decisive step forward so they had no choice but to follow him.

After a few paces they came into a circular section of the room with three archways leading in a different direction. It would have been weird if they hadn't heard voices coming from two of them and headed towards the nearest. This led them around a corner and into a dungeon style room, which was actually the bar. The next doorway they later discovered was the toilets and the last was the dining hall, where the festivities would take place. The circular room connecting them would later turn into a dance floor.

"I like this place already!" Nick said, maneuvering Jo towards the bar.

Laura looked around the dimly lit room, but didn't recognise anyone she knew; they were all her sister's friends. She was anxious to explore their surroundings because it was a magical atmosphere just being in a historical building; Laura could feel herself being pulled in.

"I'll save your drink, if you want to look around," Nick offered, knowing instinctively how she was feeling.

"I can wait. I don't want to abandon my date so soon."

"Date?" Nick said, feigning confusion.

"Figure of speech; companion, escort, friend, chaperone… whatever."

"Any and all of the above."

Laura looked at him; his expression was serious when it should have been light and it scared her for a moment. She instantly thought about the conversation she had with James, and his words rang in her ears.

"Hey, Blue, don't freak out on me. Who wouldn't want to be with the loveliest woman in the room?" Nick said in defense, but Laura didn't like the edge to his voice.

"One vodka martini," Jo said coming towards them, dissolving the tension.

"Look who I found." Neil entered the room with Laura's sister, Monica, and her boyfriend, Harry.

"Why aren't you wearing your masks?" Monica asked; there was mischief emanating form her every pore.

They all put their masks on and were instantly transformed by the illusion of mystery.

"I need to give you these," Monica said to the group. "I knew you wouldn't follow the rules and come in the right entrance; that would be too boring!" She handed them each a white envelope. "Don't open it until you've had further instructions."

"Will it self destruct?" Nick asked, tucking the envelope in his pocket.

"It's the ticket to something far more exiting than that!" Monica answered. "That's all I will say, except you will love it; trust me."

Eventually they moved into the next room, where a stage had been set up for the festivities. Laura's parents looked like they were attending under duress, knowing what their youngest daughter was capable of. She tried to reassure them that there would be some semblance of control if Samantha had anything to do with it, but she was secretly looking forward to a little adventure.

Laura laughed in delight when her sister got up onto the stage. She had changed her outfit and was now dressed as a court jester; the perfect message that she would have the last laugh. Phoebe went to stand beside her just as Samantha joined them on stage. The lights in the big hall flashed on and off a few times to indicate that Monica was ready to begin, all eyes turned to the stage.

"Welcome esteemed guests! I have an evening full of surprises planned for you. As most of you will know, I love games, and as this is my party I decided to organise a celebration with a difference. My sister here, will shortly run through the rules with you. I asked her help and advice because she is an expert at organising events.

I know I am supposed to be the 'birthday girl' and my family wanted the party to be a surprise, but you know me and convention. I also think too many of our family events, (sorry, mum), follow a pattern. The guests who know each other are glued to each other for fear of having to introduce themselves to someone new.

Anyway, enough about me; I will pass you over to Samantha so we can begin this evening of fun!

There was a spontaneous round of applause. Monica grinned broadly and bowed a few times before getting off the stage. Laura saw her father put his hands around her neck and pretend to throttle her. When Phoebe's voice sounded strong and confident, Laura turned her attention back to the stage.

"Hi, everyone. I'll keep it short, because we have kept you waiting long enough and I am sure you are all famished. When you first came in, you were given a number and asked to keep it a secret. Someone else in the room will have a number that corresponds with yours. In a moment I will ask you to take out your number and find the person you are paired with. This person will become your team mate for the evening. The first thing you will do is find your positions in the dining hall. You will be sat together and should take this opportunity to get to know each other better – if you know each other at all."

Murmurs of interest and excitement spread through the crowd, making it difficult to hear Phoebe. She indicated this to Samantha who paused until she had everyone's attention again.

"I will let you know after the meal what happens next. For now I would just like to say, 'Happy Birthday, little sister, enjoy your night'. Everyone please now find the person with the same number you hold. Let the games begin."

Laura took out her number and scanned the crowd; people were chatting animatedly, looking forward to what lay ahead. As she was searching for her team mate, she spotted Nick across the room. He looked uncomfortable behind his mask, like he wished it could really hide him from the people he didn't want to see. Nick was a confident man, but he didn't like to be in the spotlight; at any other function, he was happy to blend into the background. For a man of his size, that was never easy. Now, with a few people hoping he would be their number one man this evening, he was probably starting to wish he was dressed more conspicuously. Laura smiled at him in sympathy when he met her gaze, rolling her eyes and shrugging slightly. Nick grinned at her, bowing dramatically.

"Catch you later?" Laura signed.

"Definitely," he signed back, winking as he moved away into the crowd. It was easy to see which direction he went; he was taller than most people in the room, and a domineering sight. He had certainly changed from the gangly teenager who hid himself behind a mop of dark hair.

"Excuse me?" a soft spoken voice came from behind her. Turning, Laura saw a young woman who looked a similar age to her sister.

"Are you number 25 by any chance?"

Laura smiled. "As a matter of fact I am," she replied. "Hi, my name is Laura."

"I'm Suzie, I go to university with your sister," she answered, breaking eye contact and looking over Laura's shoulder.

"Do you know him?" she gestured with her head. For a moment Laura had no idea what she was talking about.

"The hunk by the stage." Laura looked back and saw Nick standing with Jo, trying to dodge Monica who would never knowingly allow them to pair up.

"Yes, he's one of my closest friends," Laura told Suzie.

"How lucky are you? I wish I got to look at a vision like that on a regular basis!" Suzie enthused, unable to take her eyes off Nick.

"I have to pinch myself daily!" Laura quipped, bringing Suzie's attention back to her.

"Any chance of an introduction?" she asked grinning.

"Maybe later, right now we have to eat. I have a feeling we will need our strength if my sister has anything to do with it."

"Cool!"

Laura didn't get another chance to speak to Nick or Jo during the meal. She occasionally caught their attention; or rather Nick caught hers by pulling a face. At one point he distracted Laura so much that she lost valuable points in a game.

Jo had somehow managed to bribe Monica into letting them pair up, whilst Neil was entertained by Grandma Kane. He was having a ball; she was the life and soul of any party and probably the best person to be paired with. Jo and Nick on the other hand argued constantly because they both had a huge competitive streak.

Laura had fun with Suzie. They didn't win many of the games, but they gave it their best shot, so neither took it to heart. Towards the end of the evening Samantha asked everyone to gather round the stage and Monica was presented with her birthday gifts from the family. Of course, her little sister lavished the attention, and Laura was thrilled that the evening had been a success.

Following Jo's path to the ladies room, Laura was a feeling a little merry, though it was more to do with the atmosphere than the alcohol she had consumed. She found herself in the circular section that would presumably soon become a dance floor, and waited until her eyes adjusted. As she approached the archway that led to the ladies, she paused when she saw a shadow looming towards her.

Nick almost collided with her as he strode purposely around the corner. Laura put her hand out to stop him; it was like making contact with a brick wall.

"Sorry," Nick laughed, taking hold of her hand.

"Where are you going in such a hurry?"

"I just need to do something and I was trying to build up the courage to see it through," Nick whispered, she could tell he was nervous and for some reason it frightened her.

"What do you need to do?" she asked, somehow knowing that it involved her. Nick was silent for a few seconds; it seemed like an eternity to Laura.

"What's wrong…?" Without warning, Nick cupped her face with his hands and silenced her with a kiss. Laura tensed, so shocked that at first she didn't know how to react. When Nick pulled her to him in a closer embrace, her lips moved against his with a frightening kind of familiarity. Laura's head began to spin; she had felt the kiss before.

When she brought her hand up to touch his face, it was almost like breaking a spell; he jumped back immediately - she would have fallen if he hadn't put an arm out to catch her. Laura looked up at Nick, who was staring down at her in shock; his eyes almost black. For the first time she could not read them. They stood facing each other, neither of them moving, neither saying a word.

"I might have known I couldn't keep you two apart!" Monica said as she approached, finally breaking the silence.

"It's my irresistible charm," Nick said weakly, never taking his eyes off Laura.

"Kind of why I'm here. I've been looking all over for you; your friend here promised to introduce her team mate to you, she's kind of smitten," Monica told him. She didn't seem to notice the tension between them. Laura just wanted her to leave, but instead Suzie appeared by her side.

"Excuse me," Laura said suddenly. "I have to get some air." She didn't wait for a response. Practically running in the opposite direction, she searched blindly for an exit. She finally saw a door in front of her, and headed towards it. She didn't notice Jo was heading to cut her off.

"Not right now, Jo. I just need to be alone for a minute," Laura said when she stepped in front of her, blocking the exit.

"I'll come to find you soon," Jo said quietly.

"Nick may need you," Laura said. She walked around her without saying anything further, and rushed out of the room.

She stumbled into a small courtyard that looked like a secret garden from another world. It was a beautiful scene lit by moonlight, but she was numbed to everything, including her idyllic surroundings.

The feelings fighting for attention inside her were a mixture of disbelief, confusion, anxiety and dread. She sank onto a bench, unaware that she had company until a voice spoke to her in the semi-darkness.

"Great party!"

Laura turned slowly, not recognising her male companion. "It was," Laura replied without thinking.

"Oh, I'm sure it still is; just maybe not for you at this moment in time." His directness surprised her, it sounded like something Nick would say. Or perhaps that was just because her head was full of him.

"What happened to spoil your fun?" he asked beside her.

Laura said nothing. She did not know this man, yet she had an urge to talk to him about it.

"I'm not sure where to start, it is difficult to explain."

"What's difficult? Something caused you to run out of there like you were fleeing a burning building."

"My best friend just changed my life forever. That may sound like a complete exaggeration to you, but when Nick kissed me he changed our relationship and I feel like he…" Laura couldn't finish, she wasn't even making sense. Her words were as incoherent as the thoughts that were dancing in her head.

"So, your relationship changed. What is so bad about that?" the man asked.

"We have been friends since we were… well since forever. He is the one constant that I have always been able to rely on. That kiss has changed everything. He wouldn't just kiss me on a whim and it's not the first time; though that time I didn't know it was him." Laura closed her eyes and fought back the tears. "I'm sorry," she said after awhile. "You don't even know me and I'm sharing intimate details with you. You probably came out here for some peace and quiet, but instead you get a hysterical woman!"

"If I hadn't wanted to know I wouldn't have asked. You looked like you needed to get something off your chest and I happen to have a very good ear," her companion said.

There was a moment of silence, it should have felt awkward, but she was strangely comforted in his presence.

"Did you enjoy the kiss?"

Laura looked across at him. "What difference does that make? It's a little more complicated than that."

"Only if you want it to be. You have been friends for a long time and now your relationship is about to change. If you didn't enjoy the kiss then you try to work something out – I'm sure you've been through worse. If you enjoyed it on the other hand, I can't see anything wrong with that."

Laura laughed despite herself. If only life could be that simple; yet she didn't feel as hopeless as she had five minutes ago.

"Think about it," he said, rising to his feet.

"I will."

Laura watched him leave, wondering who he was. It was by far, the strangest conversation she'd ever had. They almost didn't need to make things personal. Their encounter and his departure seemed natural yet unreal at the same time. She could have been speaking her thoughts out loud. They hadn't exchanged names, or any of the usual introductory openers, in fact nothing about their conversation had followed social norms.

Returning to the bench beside Laura, the Guardian watched her staring after his previous form and knew she was analysing the exchange. Knowing her as well as he did, he also knew exactly what to say when she sat beside him; what she did now was out of his hands. He needed her to start thinking rationally instead of emotionally and the only way he knew how to do that, was to cut through the shock by making her think about the basics; it was certainly a place to start. He could sense her confusion; even now a storm was brewing inside her. The Guardian hoped she could hold it at bay long enough to see to the heart of the matter.

He laid his hand on her shoulder to try and calm her; it had worked in the past. Laura was not a selfish person, she wasn't self absorbed or incapable of empathy, yet sometimes people who knew her questioned the blindness she had around Nick.

The Guardian tried his best earlier, by knocking a box from the top shelf of her wardrobe, he hoped that she would start to remember her earlier life with Nick and the pieces would start to fit. She hadn't been ready to face what she needed to. He knew that when she read the assignment describing her soul mate. Who that was should have been obvious, but Laura was too close and she couldn't see what he knew to be true. Nick had been brave to make a move; his method was a little unusual, but his motives pure.

Laura shifted on the bench. He could see from her posture that she was beginning to get cold. As if on cue, she shivered and rubbed her arms. The Guardian watched her closely as she began to fiddle with her wedding band. She could not bring herself to remove it, though she had moved it to her other hand; a huge step at the time. Laura was no doubt wondering how Matt would feel about it.

"You can do this," he whispered softly in encouragement; his words caressing her like the breeze. It took a long moment, but finally Laura stood; a look of determination on her face. The Guardian rose too, and stood beside her. When she moved towards the entrance, he walked with her.

When Laura re-entered the grand hall she was feeling a little dizzy, and realised she had been holding her breath. She saw Nick immediately; the sight of him brought her to a standstill. His ability to do that was at least familiar to her, but the rest was foreign territory. Being with him had always been so natural, but now she was terrified at the prospect of walking towards him.

Laura felt rooted to the spot; inside she was debating whether to back up and return to the garden or continue towards her friend. It was then that he looked at her, and the expression on his beautiful face robbed whatever breath she had left in her body. Laura couldn't stand to see so much pain and insecurity in his eyes and she knew what she needed to do.

With renewed determination, Laura moved forward again. Nick must have seen the intent in her gaze, because as she reached him he raised his eyebrows in question. Before she could change her mind, Laura grabbed the lapels of his jacket and pulled him towards her; it was the only thing she could think of, save standing on a chair.

As her lips met his she saw the surprise in his eyes, but he kissed her back. There was an urgency in Laura that she couldn't explain. Her mouth crushed his, as she moved closer to him.

Nick didn't disappoint her; he pulled her towards him, wrapping his arms tightly around her. The kiss was over far too quickly, and Laura looked at Nick with disappointment as he held her away from him. She still couldn't read his eyes. It was a new side to him and she was in un-chartered waters.

"Let's get out of here," Nick said hoarsely, taking her hand and leading her across the hall. Laura didn't protest, she was working on pure instinct now, which filled her with a nervous energy. As she passed Jo, she easily read the expression on her face; it said 'don't hurt him'.

"It will be all right," she mouthed at her friend; receiving a nod in return.

As they stepped into fresh air, Laura saw that the Limousine they arrived in was still waiting; she allowed Nick to guide her towards it. He hadn't said a word as they marched through the castle. His silence made her a little apprehensive but she didn't want to break the spell by saying anything. As they sat beside one another in the car, presumably on the way back to her flat, Laura hardly recognised herself or her friend. She wasn't as comfortable as she had been earlier, trying on the mask in front of the mirror, but she wasn't afraid.

She looked at Nick's profile and her heart began to flutter in her chest. She hadn't felt like that in a long time; it was intoxicating. Laura couldn't help wondering how she could have looked at his familiar face for so long and not seen what she was seeing now. Nick didn't turn to look at her, though he must have been aware of her attention. Instead he squeezed her hand.

For a moment, Laura wondered if she was doing the right thing. They had been friends for a long time, and she didn't want to do anything to jeopardise that. But when she saw his face at the party, it was almost like he lifted a mask and all his feelings were laid bare. The look was enough to take her breath away. When James told her that Nick had feelings for her, she had scoffed; she couldn't imagine their relationship being anything but platonic. Yet, when she kissed him, she felt something that had nothing to do the affection of a friend, and she wanted to explore that. Something in her gut told her that by giving it a chance, she had nothing to lose.

"Thank you," Nick said to the driver, and Laura realised with shock that they had arrived. Again, Nick led the way. He grasped her hand tighter and pulled her up the steps towards her flat with renewed purpose.

It wasn't until they were over the threshold that he let go of her hand. It felt cold for a moment, and Laura unconsciously folded it under her arm.

Finally Nick met her gaze. "We need to talk," he said to her. "I suppose you have a lot of questions and are a little confused right now."

"Yes, on both counts," Laura answered moving towards him. "But we have been talking for almost thirty years - the talking can wait."

Nick looked at her, amused for a moment. He must have seen the apprehension on her face, because the humour quickly vanished and he filled the distance between them. This time when he kissed her his lips were gentle, his mouth exploring hers; eradicating any doubts in Laura's mind.

"Nicky," she whispered when they finally came up for air.

Pushing her away again, he looked into her eyes. "Don't say my name like that, Laura, unless you truly want this to happen, unless you have no doubts that this is what you want."

"Nicky," Laura said again.

Nick pulled her to him. He lifted her off the ground and hugged her to him, burying his face in her hair. Laura could feel his heart beating against her own chest; its rhythm in time with hers.

"What are you afraid of?" she asked him, when he finally put her down, but made no move to kiss her again.

"I'm afraid of how you are making me feel, especially when you kiss me the way you did at the party. I'm afraid that you haven't had enough time to think about this, but most of all, I've wanted you for so long that I am terrified of losing control."

Laura put her hand on his face and smiled up at him. "So what if you lose control. I haven't seen this side of you, but I like it so far!" she told him.

Nick looked at her, still fighting what he wanted.

"Will you kiss me already?" Laura sighed, her thumb caressing his mouth. Nick groaned, closing his eyes briefly. When he opened them again, Laura saw such need in their depths that her breath caught in her throat.

This time, Nick lowered his head and brushed his lips against hers; all the uncertainty gone. As they clung to each other, matching need for need, Laura could think of nothing else. At that moment, it felt so right, that she abandoned herself completely.

Laura opened her eyes and looked around her. She had dozed off after making love to Nick. Her eyes rested on his body. For a moment she was embarrassed; she had never seen him naked before. Smiling at her own silliness, Laura's eyes traveled up his body admiringly, until they came to rest on his face. When she realised Nick was watching her, she blushed a bright crimson.

"Don't be embarrassed, I like it when you look at me that way," he said, leaning forward and kissing her on the nose. "How do you feel?"

"I feel surprisingly calm, after some of the things I've just done with my best friend - and liked a lot!"

Nick laughed at her comment, continuing to plant kisses on her face. "I'm glad to hear it."

"I take it that talk will have to wait a little while longer?" Laura commented as he started moving down her neck.

"A few days should do it!" Nick whispered between kisses.

"I was wrong before," Laura said on a moan, as Nick continued to work his way down her body. "I don't like this new side of you - I love it."

Nick chuckled, tickling her skin. Laura moved underneath him, completely awake now.

"Do you know what I love most of all?" she asked as he made his way back up to her mouth.

"What?" Nick asked, far too busy concentrating on her body.

"The colour of your eyes when you look at me the way you are doing right now."

"Tell me about the colour of my eyes," Nick murmured, as he teased her mouth with his; his hands traveling the path he had just marked out with kisses.

"Not fair," Laura whispered, losing her chain of thought.

"Since when did I ever play fair?"

Laura laughed, tipping him over whilst she had the advantage, and moving her position on top of him.

"I'm familiar with the colour when you are angry," she said, leaning to kiss his neck. "When you're sad." Nick sighed in pleasure when her mouth started a journey of its own. "Happy." Laura rubbed herself against him and returned her mouth to his lips to catch a moan. "Mischievous." Her own eyes twinkled now, as her hands began to roam his body.

"I get the picture," Nick said breathlessly, grinning at her. "You play dirty too."

"When you are aroused."

"Kind of like now?" Nick said flipping her back over.

"Exactly like now. That colour is best of…" he silenced her with another kiss, and this time Laura didn't say another word for quite some time.

"Is this weird to you?" Laura asked Nick in the early hours of the morning, as they lay facing each other.

"It feels like the most natural thing in the world, but I guess weird in the sense that I keep thinking I'm going to wake up," Nick told her.

"When you first kissed me, I kind of freaked out for a while; though admittedly nothing compared to my usual standards!" Laura said. Nick smiled at her, saying nothing. "I had so many questions. But they somehow seem insignificant now."

"That's because you want my body!" Nick joked.

"That's true. I cannot believe I'm still aroused. Being with you like this feels so natural," Laura said honestly, brushing a stray hair out of his eyes.

"I will answer all your questions, because believe me, when you start to analyse this I will be bombarded," Nick teased.

Laura hit him over the head with a pillow. "Why didn't you ever tell me?" she asked.

"It's such a long story, and there have been so many reasons along the way."

"And you accuse me of being a drama queen," Laura said, pushing herself up onto her elbow.

"Let me put it this way, I have known there was only one woman for me since she first covered me in poster paint!"

Laura felt bad when he said that; she should have known how he felt; she didn't understand why she hadn't.

"Don't look at me like that, Blue," he whispered stroking her face. "I didn't know until we were in high school that my feelings for you had changed. I have to admit that it was difficult for me when you met Matt, but my feelings were very new and having you in my life was more important than spoiling what we had. I have loved having you as a friend and I knew that I couldn't have all of you; for a long time that was enough." Nick paused, brushing the tears in her eyes. "I was happy with our relationship. Seeing you so happy made me realise that I had to be thankful for what I had. Then I met Zoe, and I was in love with her in the beginning, until our differences came between us. I was afraid of losing you if I told you. You are, and always have been, one of the most important people in my life. I've always had a part of you that no-one else had, not even Matt, and I didn't want to lose that."

Laura smiled at him through her tears. "What changed your mind?" she asked.

"I think maybe because of how close we've been this past year, and I started to hope that things could be different between us. I've never allowed myself to do that before." Nick stroked her face gently. "When you met James, I was consumed with a jealousy that I didn't know I was capable of. I didn't like myself, but I felt I was losing what little chance I had, so I began to push you away."

"I can't believe I was so stupid. I really had no idea what you were feeling and why you were behaving that way."

"You were going through an emotional time," Nick said.

"No, don't make excuses and don't pretend you didn't think the same thing. How can I know you so well and not know how you felt?"

"You're right, I did wonder why this was the only thing I could keep from you, I've never been able to hide anything else."

"I don't know why. I know that I would never do anything to hurt you. I just never thought about our relationship being anything else."

"How do you feel now?" Nick asked her.

"Like I've been denying myself something very special." Laura saw the look of relief cross his face. "I realised something else a little while ago. I want to show you something."

"Sounds interesting," Nick said suggestively.

"Stay there, funny guy, I'll just go get it."

Laura walked to the kitchen table where she had left the box earlier. She picked up the school file and took it back to the bedroom. She showed it to Nick, sitting patiently as he read.

When he finished he put the file down and looked at her in amazement. "You were describing me," he said.

"Yes, though I didn't know it then. What I realised is that you are my soul mate Nick, we fit."

Nick pulled her to him, hugging her close. "Please tell me this isn't a dream," he whispered against her shoulder.

"It isn't a dream. It is a new reality perhaps, but one I'm looking forward to sharing with you."

"I'm going to love every minute of it," Nick agreed. "Starting right now."

As he pushed her back onto the bed Laura smiled. "Definitely the best colour of all," she sighed, wrapping her arms around him.

Chapter Twenty

Dear Sonia

You do not know me, though we have met, briefly. Who I am is not particularly important; it will not help to deliver the message. This letter is an apology of sorts. It took me a while to write it, because I wanted to make sure my motives were pure. I've mentioned that we met, and on that occasion I felt the depth of your pain. Instead of trying to help I did the cowardly thing and ran from it…

James removed his pen from the paper and looked at the words with a mixture of helplessness and despair. He screwed the paper into a ball and threw his latest attempt at a letter into the trashcan; by now spilling its contents onto the floor. He had suffered from writer's block before, but not to the extent that every word tumbled awkwardly from him; mocking him for his absurdity.

James didn't feel like he was in control anymore, and he didn't like it. Before his experiences with Laura he would never have contemplated writing a letter to a complete stranger. He wondered if the idea came to him because it was how the craziness started; he was fine until someone decided to use him like a puppet.

James looked down at the blank page and finally accepted defeat; there would be no constructive material flowing through his fingers anytime soon. He left his study. What had previously been his sanctuary, now felt like a prison, and he needed air. He took the steps two at a time as he hurried down the stairs and headed for the kitchen to retrieve his car keys. The thought struck him that perhaps he should share his feelings before they got any worse. He had talked the subject to death with his sister; though she felt sympathy for Sonia, she thought he should let it go. James on the other hand, needed closure; a compulsion to try and find the answers that he was looking for. Why, for example, he had been drawn to a stranger if nothing was to come of it. The fact that he had a sensitivity to people's emotions had never scared him so much. On the other hand, admitting that Laura's husband was communicating to her through his writing was a difficult pill to swallow.

What James feared though, more than anything that had happened so far, was to live in a world where uncertainty became the norm. He liked that he questioned things, so settling for an explanation because he couldn't find a better solution was not how he wanted to live his life.

Working purely on instinct now, he tapped Laura's number into his mobile phone. He was disappointed when the answering machine kicked in and ended the call without leaving a message. James glanced at the clock, wondering if he should try the office phone; Laura occasionally worked late and it was only 6:30 pm. He decided to try his luck. This time when he heard the mechanical tone of a machine, he cursed under his breath. He didn't hang up this time; something told him to see the call through. When he heard the beeps, James spoke with as much confidence as he could muster.

"Hi, Laura, it's James. I know we're not all workaholics, but I just wanted to chat, so called on the off chance. If you are there…"

"James, hello, this is Phoebe," a voice interrupted him.

"Oh, hello, Phoebe – you probably gathered I was hoping to speak to Laura." James felt a little foolish now.

"Only me here I'm afraid. I'm killing time in the office until my evening job starts."

"Sorry to bother you. I will try Laura again tomorrow," James said, trying to hide the disappointment.

"No, problem…" There was a slight pause before Phoebe added, "Forgive me for being direct, but are you all right?"

"Why do you ask?"

"You just sound different, maybe even a little sad," Phoebe told him, her voice was a little unsure now.

"I suppose you're used to detecting subtle changes in tone?"

"Yes, I suppose I am," she agreed.

"I'm a little stressed at the moment, that's all," James said, sitting down at the kitchen table. "Nothing I can't handle."

"That's good… I apologise if I'm being forward, we don't know each other that well after all."

"No problem, I'm sure that will change."

"That's right. I suppose it will have to if we're going to start a family together!" Phoebe said, tongue in cheek.

James laughed. "Ah, so you still want to marry me and have my babies!"

"Of course, I'm not so fickle."

"Then I guess we'll have to work on it," James said, perking up a little.

"I'm glad that's sorted. I will let Laura know you called."

"Thanks, Phoebe."

James ended the call, shaking his head in bewilderment; life was certainly full of surprises. He thought of Phoebe with her wild red hair, and spirit to match. He had never known a woman as confident, like she was completely comfortable in her own skin. He had met outspoken, dominant women before, but Phoebe seemed to burn a little bit brighter than the rest. Just thinking of her made him smile; he realized that the phone call hadn't been a complete waste of time. He had been distracted from his problems, if only for a short time.

James walked down the hall, grabbed his jacket from the peg and threw his car keys on the side. He usually felt better after a nice brisk walk to clear his head. As he walked, his thoughts turned to Laura, and what a blessing it was that they met. She was a calming influence, and he soon relaxed as he strolled down the avenue leading to the park. James agreed with Barry's philosophy that people meet for a reason; he would always be thankful that his path had crossed with hers. Although he confused his feelings for her with the connection they had, he wouldn't be human if he didn't wish they could be more than friends; she was a beautiful woman. He was also realistic, and what he felt in Nick's presence, no matter how brief, made him realise he could not compete even if he wanted to.

Ahead of him, children were playing happily on the cricket field. James sat down on a bench to watch them for a moment. He loved the innocence of children, the absolute pleasure they found in the simple things. He was looking forward to building a relationship with Eric. James could see himself taking his nephew on grand adventures and re-discovering the child within. As he watched the children he thought of Phoebe again, and her jokes about starting a family. It was a natural connection, but it made him smile even so. An image of children with bright red hair running around the field popped into James's head and his smile deepened.

The image disappeared almost as quickly when it became obvious that the two women standing a couple of feet from James were talking about the young nurse, Sonia. James slid across the bench so he could hear them more clearly.

"The thing that annoys me in situations like that, is the waste of our resources," one of the women said.

"If that nurse had been serious about suicide, then why attempt it in a place that was bound to get her noticed?" the other one agreed.

"It said in the paper though, that she lost a child - that's tough. I had a miscarriage before Tommy."

James tuned out of the conversation; he'd heard enough to make him realise what he needed to do. He knew how he could help Sonia. He would write an article to raise awareness and help people like her, who were suffering a similar loss. It would take some work; James would have to pull a few strings. The story had worn itself out by now - it was 'old news'. But he felt what she felt, if only for a moment. He also knew that if people got a taste of that, he would not only be able to reach them, he would be able to reach her too.

A pair of unblinking eyes surveyed James with what looked like interest, as he balanced his nephew on one arm in the baby bath. He was nervous; he had no experience with babies, but Eric was a trusting soul.

"I read the article you wrote on suicide," James's brother said, walking into the lounge with a glass of wine.

"You read it before it was published anyway!" James never took his eyes off the baby.

"It was very powerful; your best piece of work," Dennis said. "As for proof-reading the original, I still don't know why you insist on sending your articles to me. You don't need to."

"Are you saying you don't enjoy getting them first hand?" James asked his brother.

"Of course not!"

"Then why change the habit of a lifetime?" he asked, making a face at Eric. "I'm glad you enjoyed it, it was more important to me than usual." James looked up briefly to smile at Dennis.

"All right, Uncle James, it's time to come out now," Danielle said, joining them.

James lifted his nephew carefully out of the tub and handed him to Danielle, who had a towel ready. "That was fun," he said stroking Eric's head.

Danielle nodded, wrapping her son into a tight little bundle. "He does love the attention."

"Have you seen Laura recently?" Dennis asked.

"No, but I'm meeting her for coffee tomorrow."

"That's nice."

"Yes, I'm looking forward to it."

"So, tell us more about your friend's revelation. It's an intriguing turn of events," Danielle said.

"There isn't much to tell about Barry, I almost feel like I dreamt it! It's is rare to have a moment when he's not joking around."

Danielle smiled. "That's just who Barry is. He should have been on the stage; an excellent avenue for his talent.

"Does he know everything now?" Dennis asked.

"Yes, we've talked for a while about things. He's a good friend."

"What did he think about the article?" Dennis was interested to know.

"I'm sure he liked it, though I didn't get a straight answer. He sent me a text message about becoming psychic investigators or something like that."

"Well, you certainly seem more relaxed about everything." Danielle observed.

James nodded; he felt better since writing the article, but his family helped. He enjoyed being in their company, it was an instant pick me up.

"Dinner is ready. Shall I take Eric for a nap?" George asked, as he came out of the kitchen bearing an apron on.

"That would be great, Hon," Danielle answered. She buttoned the last of Eric's sleep suit, and passed him to his father. George was in his element, being at home with his wife and new-born son, after spending so much time off shore. He was a giving man, and James could see that he adored his sister. In the coming years, he would give her all the support she needed, and be an excellent role model for Eric.

James followed Dennis into the dining room. He felt safe in a way he hadn't felt for a long time. His uncertainties did not haunt him as much as they once had, and he looked forward to the future, no matter how strange. When George returned, he helped Danielle to serve the food. Dennis poured the wine, and James chatted easily with his sister in law, Nina, who finally made it out of the kitchen. The room was soon a hive of activity as the family dished the food and chatted in unison. They took these opportunities to catch up on each others lives; it was a close unit and they drew strength from these moments. The only people missing were there parents; who were taking a well earned break.

As they ate, James began to chew over the things they discussed. He had tried so hard in the past to get this atmosphere on paper, through his writing, but no amount of words could do it justice.

James sat in the interpreting office, waiting for Laura to complete her call. The team was out today, either on a job or grabbing a quick lunch before they began again. Laura stuck her head out of the office briefly to indicate that she wouldn't be long. That had been fifteen minutes ago, and James could hear her even through the door, talking animatedly to her caller.

"Can I get you a coffee, James?" Rebecca asked from her own office.

"I never say no to coffee!" he replied with a smile.

"Neither do I," he heard a familiar voice say. When the outer office door opened, he grinned up at Phoebe from his vantage point in the seating area.

"Good afternoon," she said with a smile. Her hair was tied back in a bun, but it still refused to be tamed completely. It was definitely her crowning glory; James denied anyone not to be mesmerised by it.

"Hi, Phoebe," he said casually.

"Chief keeping you waiting as usual?" Her tone was light so he could tell it was not a criticism.

"I know how she gets on the phone. I could be in for a long wait," James replied.

"Well that's not so bad; you can entertain me in the mean time."

"I think it's likely to be the other way around."

Phoebe winked at him, as she shrugged out of her coat. In one swift movement she hung it on a peg with one hand and opened the door with the other, as Rebecca tapped on the glass.

"Thanks, Sweetie," she said taking two cups from her.

"Not a problem," Rebecca answered, nodding in James's direction before the door closed.

"That woman is a godsend," Phoebe commented, sitting down next to James. He took the cup she offered gratefully.

"I'm sure she knows how much you appreciate her," James answered.

"I hope so; she has to put up with a lot. Rebecca is the glue that keeps us together. She listens to us rant after an assignment or about each other when we need to let off steam. She also has to carry around a huge amount of information, which is often more of a burden than a help." Phoebe had lowered her voice slightly so she didn't embarrass her colleague.

"A regular wonder woman, I should do a piece on her for *Moment In Time*," James said, only half joking.

"I would applaud the idea, but she would hate it. We will just have to let her carry on being the silent hero!"

James laughed at the comment, trying to imagine what Rebecca would say about the description.

"You seem brighter today," Phoebe observed, as she sipped her coffee.

"Do I?" he asked with interest.

"I'm doing it again aren't I? Overstepping boundaries?"

"Of course not," James reassured her. "I've been finding ways to relieve my stress recently, so you're right in that respect."

Phoebe nodded as though she knew exactly what he was talking about. He realised that he liked her more every time they met; she was one of those people in life who had great charisma. It felt good to be around her, which made sense from the things Laura said.

The door to Laura's office opened, and she came out in a rush of apologies. "James, I'm so sorry I took so long." She looked at Phoebe. "Hi, hon."

"No problem. It hasn't been so bad this waiting game," James answered winking at Phoebe.

"Good, I don't feel as guilty then." Laura laughed. "How did this morning go?" She turned to Phoebe.

"Great, thanks. I'll tell you about it later or you'll never get off to lunch."

"Fair enough," Laura answered, reaching for her jacket.

James got up and walked to join her. "Nice seeing you again, Phoebe," he said.

"You too."

"See you soon Phoebes," Laura added, opening the door.

As James was about to go through it, Phoebe called him back. "About these children - do you want one of each or both the same sex?" she asked.

"Oh, I was thinking more like four or five, but perhaps we'd better start with a date."

As the door closed behind him, James heard Phoebe giggle in delight. "Like I said, you're adorable!" she shouted after him.

Laura shook her head as they walked on, she didn't seem surprised by Phoebe's goading. "I think she genuinely likes you," she told James.

"And here I am thinking she wants to marry every man she meets!"

Laura smiled. "A mutual attraction."

"She's a lot of fun."

"I couldn't agree more, but enough about your associations with members of my staff. Where do you want to eat?"

"The same place as last time?" James suggested, remembering that they did a killer Banoffee Pie.

Laura was distracted for a moment as she tried to dodge a wasp; her movements looked like part of some alternative dance routine.

"It's not a tiger!" James said, trying hard not to laugh.

Laura smiled, a little embarrassed, but relieved the wasp had grown bored with the game and moved on. "Let's go, before he brings back some of his friends for the entertainment value!"

They chatted as they walked. Laura asked him questions about his article; she had liked it, which meant a lot. It had been a while since they'd talked on the phone. James could feel the intensity of their earlier relationship wearing off. It didn't concern him; he knew that they would remain firm friends. They had a connection now, and even if his feelings had changed, she was still important to him.

"Did Barry ever tell you about the reoccurring dream he had about you?" Laura asked when they had chosen a seat in the café.

"Yes, as a matter of fact he did. He said that we were having a conversation and he couldn't understand what I was saying - he said I was speaking in a foreign tongue."

"How interesting," Laura commented.

"I know. He also dreamt that when I became frustrated that he couldn't understand me, I started scribbling on pieces of paper. Pretty soon I was consumed by a pile of stationery which all had words only I could read."

"That is pretty amazing," Laura exclaimed. "This whole thing has been one weird journey." "Life changing, literally," James agreed. "And talking of changes - how is it going with Nick?"

Laura blushed, which he found incredibly endearing.

"That good?"

She laughed self consciously, recovering from her initial embarrassment. "You have no idea!"

Laura told him that Nick was still skeptical about the letters, but that he accepted her explanation. She briefly touched on James's ability to read people, using an analogy Nick could understand. James wasn't a science-fiction fan per say, but he did find being characterized as an *'empath demon'*, or something along those lines, pretty amusing.

As usual, any time spent with Laura, whether seeing her in person or chatting on the phone, passed far too quickly. Before he knew it, it was time for them to return to work.

"So, you are doing okay?" Laura asked as they walked back to the office.

"I'm doing okay. Overall, the past month or so has been a positive experience. I can start dealing with the issues as they arise."

"And you know where I am?" Laura said.

"I won't let you forget it!" he said, his tone light.

"I know I've already told you this many times, but I'm glad we met," she told him.

"Me too." James didn't say anything more than that. He didn't need to.

Chapter Twenty-one

From: Joanna@terpterp.org.uk

To: lauraBSL@interpreter.co.uk

Subject: Hi stranger!

I haven't heard from you in a while. I'm guessing you are busy with 'Mr. Lover Lover' (sorry for the Shaggy reference – you started it by calling him 'Mr. Fantastic'!).

I was going to ring, but it got too late when we were finally through with the latest conference gig. It was actually quite exciting – I gave a presentation on interpreting in international sign.

Anyway, I'll fill you in later. I just wanted to let you know that I am home next month for your birthday.

Can you arrange something, (I know that's cheeky because it's your birthday), but we will be doing the whole family thing and I wanted to make sure the terrible trio got together at last, (that's you, me and Nicky – in case you've forgotten!).

Have a think about it and give me a ring.

Love ya

Jo

Laura re-read her email; it was the third time she had taken in the information, almost as if she wanted to savour it: programme it into her memory. She had always enjoyed receiving mail from Jo. Every so often a letter came in the post and she would carry it with her for days, reading her favourite parts and sharing her friend's life through her words.

There used to be a time when they saw one another every day; as school children they had giggled into their text books when they were meant to be working, and they still giggled like teenagers whenever they were together.

Laura pressed the reply button and was about to write a message when the telephone interrupted her task. She glanced at the clock, wondering whether to answer it. She had arrived at work early, and it was still only 8 am. She picked up the receiver. "Hello, Laura Kane speaking. How may I help?"

"Laura, thank goodness I didn't get the machine," Gary said; something in his tone alerted her.

"Gary, what a pleasant surprise," she replied, forcing enthusiasm into her voice.

"I wish this call was under better circumstances." He began. "But I'm afraid I must be the bearer of bad news. Charlie's father passed away last night."

"Oh, Gary, I'm so sorry to hear that," Laura said, her heart aching for Charlie and her family.

There was a silence then, as he searched for more words.

"Please let me know if there is anything I can do, and give my love to Charlie. I will be thinking of you all," Laura said, feeling very sad.

Gary choked up. "Thanks, Laura."

"No problem, honey. You take good care."

"I will."

When she replaced the handset, Laura sat for a moment her thoughts on Charlie. It was hard to imagine what she was going through right now. When she lost Matt, those first few days were a blur of painful memories.

Nick's face came into her mind then and she stood abruptly. If he didn't already know, she needed to tell him, and if he did, he would need her support.

She grabbed her bag, and left the office, only stopping to lock the door and write a message for Rebecca on her way out. She had two hours before her first assignment, and she wanted to be with Nick until then.

It took Laura longer than she anticipated toreach Nick's house; the rush hour and traffic lights contending to slow her speed. When she finally arrived and pushed the door bell anxiously, Nick answered it in a matter of seconds.

"You heard then?" he said, more in statement than in question.

"Yes, Gary phoned. I came straight over," Laura answered, stepping over the threshold to hug him. His hair was wet and he smelt delicious from a recent shower. She was slightly embarrassed that under the circumstances the smell aroused her, but Nick didn't seem to notice. He leaned down and kissed her softly on the forehead.

"Thanks for coming, Blue," he whispered.

Laura followed him to the couch and sat down next to him. He told her that Charlie had sent a text message in the early hours. It was the only way she was able to tell him, and he understood that, but he hated the cold, almost mechanical feel of replying by mobile phone.

"I just feel so helpless. I don't know what to do, or even what to say," Nick explained.

"I know it's difficult and in truth there is nothing that you can say to make it any easier for her, but it is the little things that are important," Laura told him, taking his hand.

"The little things?" he asked.

"Yes, and they come naturally to you, even if you don't realise it. You are thinking about it too much," she said, not unkindly. "When Matt died you were amazing; you were there when I needed you without being obtrusive. Sometimes you would just sit with me without saying a word, so that I felt your warmth; other times you would cook for me or listen to me talk about him for hours."

Nick smiled at her, squeezing her hand. She looked down thoughtfully; his hand in hers had evoked another memory. "You've always been that way. I remember when we were around twelve and my grandfather died. It was the first family member we lost and the first time I experienced death. I can recall vividly how you appeared beside me in the funeral car and took my hand in yours. You didn't say anything, you didn't need to, and I took great comfort in that," Laura said, looking up at him.

"Thanks, Blue; you always know what to say. You're probably right about thinking too much. I think maybe it's because it was expected

— it's what makes it seem worse somehow. Charlie knew her father was going to die, she just didn't know how quickly."

"All you can do, Nicky, is let her know that you are there for her if she needs you. It will come naturally, you'll see. You may be an excellent surgeon in practical terms, but your consultations are a big part of what makes you an excellent doctor."

"And might we be a little bit biased?" Nick teased her.

"Completely, but it doesn't make it any less true."

Nick leaned forward and kissed her on the mouth. "You," he said between kisses, "are amazing."

Wiping a lock of hair out of his eyes, Laura smiled. "I thought we had a rule about that?" she said.

"Oh, the friendship rule."

"That's right."

"But we are more than just friends, so the rules have changed. I can now show my appreciation for the things you do for me. I bet you're supposed to be working right now," Nick said.

"I have to go in about twenty minutes," Laura agreed. "I just wanted to check in.

"Well, thanks. I have to be at work in a few hours too. My morning surgery was cancelled, so I'm going in a little later."

"Are you free tonight?"

"Yes and there's no place I'd rather be," Nick answered, as he got to his feet.

"Where are you going?"

"To pour you a coffee - you don't have much time."

Laura laughed, following him in to the kitchen.

She managed to arrive on time for her appointment, which was a good thing; she was already worrying about Charlie so she didn't need another distraction. As she was switching her phone to silent, she noticed a message had arrived from Nick. She took a few moments to look at it before she went into the courthouse. Laura laughed out loud at the words.

```
From: Nicky
I just wanted to say that I caught the look you gave me
when you arrived. I liked it xx
```

Another message had made its way into her inbox and opened by the time she had finished reading the first.

```
From: Nicky
and there is no need to be embarrassed. Apparently it
is this new aftershave... every member of the female
species, including the animal kingdom, will find me
irresistible! x
```

Laura resisted the urge to rise to the bait and instead sent a brief reply that she knew would make him smile.

```
To: Nicky
```
You're truly scrumptious truly truly scrumptious x x

Laura dropped the phone into her bag and strode towards the imposing building, inside which she would be spending most of her day.

The Guardian sat beside Laura as she prepared to interpret for a client. It was a complicated case and she had been consulting with the team for over an hour. He could feel her strength beginning to fade, as she focused on solving the latest dilemma.

"You can do this. Think about what happened in the Stringer case," he whispered to her. Though she did not verbally respond to what he said, he could feel her body begin to relax.

Of course she had been more at ease in recent weeks than she had for some time. He was relieved everything worked out well during her introduction to James. They were good for one another; they would have met again sooner of later, even without his help.

What the Guardian could now see though, were the effects on her spirit since she had discovered the truth about Nick. If their relationship had remained the same, it would not have harmed their connection; it was like a magnet that would always keep them together. But their relationship had changed; it had evolved into a rare and valuable gift. He couldn't be happier with the result of their particular union. They were both good people, and would positively affect the lives of others they knew because of their happiness, faith and love for one another. It gave them the strength to be the people they wanted to be. He knew that many people admired the bond they shared; it was a sad fact that some go their whole lives without feeling that strength of belonging, or experiencing the pure joy that comes from opening your soul to another completely.

The Guardian wished that all his assignments were as successful. There had been times when his charges had been in so much pain, it was all he could do not to despair. At those times he concentrated all his power to make sure they knew they were not alone; he spoke to their heart directly and took them to a moment in their life when they had experienced peace or joy. This helped them in their journey, and it was perhaps the only thing that kept him from questioning his existence. Humans do not have the monopoly on doubt, but thankfully the very fact that he could touch a soul, if only for a moment, reminded him of the strength and purpose of his creation.

He walked now to the recently opened door of the courtroom, and allowed a representation of himself to be seen; joining a group in the public gallery. This time he was a young woman, looking enough like Laura's sister to catch her attention. When he sat down, and turned towards her, their eyes met briefly. He took this opportunity to smile her way, a smile so genuine and without reason that she smiled back in return; the connection had been made, and until it was safe to slip away, he would offer her his guidance from this vantage point.

Chapter Twenty-two

From: C. Kemp
Hi Nicky. I am running a little late... I will be there as soon as I can - don't leave... Charlie

Nick closed his eyes and allowed the sounds of the river to wash over him. He had arranged to meet Charlie for lunch because a window had opened in his schedule - he didn't have long.

She approached so quietly that it wasn't until she sat down beside him that Nick knew she was there. He hadn't seen her in over a week so he was relieved that she did not look as fragile, though she had lost weight.

"Charlie, it's good to see you," he said, leaning over to kiss her cheek.

"Thanks. You too." Holding up a bag, Charlie smiled softly. "I brought some goodies; people are still sending us food," she said.

"How are you holding up?"

"I'm doing the best I can. It may sound strange, but I think I can now begin a healing process, not only from losing Dad, but from losing the person I was before his illness."

"It doesn't sound strange at all. I admire your strength," Nick told her.

They had spoken on the phone a few days before and she had finally been able to tell him what happened. Nick kept a low profile at the funeral, once he let her know that he was there for her. He went, even though he did not know her family, because was important to Charlie. Nick held Laura's hand throughout the service, and cried softly for a man he had never met. He knew it had a lot to do with the mortality of his own father, but he respected the man because of the picture his daughter had painted. Charlie had been with him at the end, with other members of his immediate family. She talked about the intimate, private, goodbye they shared and it tore at Nick's heart.

Looking at her now he sensed she was starting to come to terms with her loss, and allowing the grieving process to take its course.

"I'm going to really miss him you know," she whispered, as if sensing Nick's thoughts.

"I know."

"I don't think I will ever get used to him not being around. I will always carry him in here, of course." Charlie pointed to her heart. "But it isn't quite the same."

They were silent for a few moments. Charlie wiped a stray tear from her cheek, and looked out across the water. "I want to thank you for everything you've done for me, especially your support," she said, turning to Nick.

"No thanks necessary, that's what friends are for; we have helped each other," Nick pointed out.

"I know. I just needed to say it."

"It almost sounds like you're saying goodbye," he said.

"I am, in a way. I will keep in touch, but I've decided to go to Scotland. Mum is coming with me for a while, so that will be good for both of us."

"That's great," Nick said. "I'm sure it will give you the time you both need to heal."

"Yes, that's why I feel determined to make a go of it. Dad's illness hit me harder than I realised. I didn't see the classic signs of my stress until it was almost too late," Charlie whispered, it was still painful to talk about. "My depression went un-noticed for a long time because I put a brave face on for the rest of the world, even Gary. I began to disassociate myself from people, without realising I was doing it, and it drove a wedge between us." She smiled a little shyly. "I forgot how to be myself with people, everyone that is, except for you. I think it's because I didn't know you well, and because you were going through a similar thing, I could let my defenses down."

"I'm glad I could help," Nick said, touched by her words.

"You really did. But now it is time I helped myself, and hopefully save my marriage," Charlie told him with quiet determination.

"I think you can do anything you set your mind to."

"It is amazing how one event can be a chain reaction in terms of how it can affect your life."

"I know."

This silenced them again, but it was not an uncomfortable silence. They sat beside one another, not needing words to appreciate the comfort they had gained when they needed it.

Nick was not sad when it was time to leave; he felt confident that Charlie would find herself again, and knew that their relationship had served its purpose.

They would keep in touch, mainly through Laura, and that was enough for them both.

"So, when are you going to retire from the limelight and come to live in the real world?" Nick asked Jo as they sat together in his living room.

"Don't let her lull you into a false sense of security, she's been promising to spend more time at home for years," Laura said, from the throw cushion, perched at Jo's feet.

Jo smiled in triumph. "Actually, Neil and I are training a new team to take over from us... you know what I mean – mentoring or whatever."

"That's great news!" Nick said. "I don't know how we've managed without you for so long," he added winking at Laura.

"So, you two are actually going to find time for me when you're not making puppy-dog eyes at each another?"

"Puppy-dog eyes?" Laura asked.

"You know; adoring, sickly, only meant for each other!"

Nick laughed at her description; it was difficult to stop when she was around. "Well, at least I've been referred to as something other than the object of a song," he said, still laughing. "I've been '*Mr. Bombastic*' and a female character from '*Chitty, Chitty, Bang, Bang*', I'm not sure which I prefer!"

"A female character? Darling, you look a million miles away from a female character of any description," Jo protested.

This time it was Laura's turn to get the giggles. As she tried to control her laughter, she explained what Nick meant.

"That must be a Laura thing, I just don't get it!"

"You two are incorrigible!"

"Don't start, buddy. You can't say anything about a few song references – you refer any situation to a film," Jo said.

Laura struggled to get to her feet. "Speaking of which, let's organise the wine and goodies for our film fest."

Nick stood up and took her hand; pulling her gently, in one swift motion she was in a standing position.

"Thanks," she said to him gratefully.

They walked to the kitchen together, with Jo following close behind making kissing noises with her mouth.

"You are so immature!" Laura said turning to pull a face at her.

"I know. I'll be good now, I promise," Jo chuckled.

"No, you won't," Nick countered, stopping to peruse the wine collection.

"What is it tonight – red or white?"

"One of each to start with!" Jo said leaning around him and taking a bottle in each hand.

"Like you'll get through more than three glasses," Laura commented, shaking her head.

"We need something to wash all that sugar down," Jo said, looking at the collection on the counter.

"Neil is coming too. I got extra because I know what you ladies are like once you start," Nick told them.

Walking over to the goodies he started to pile bowls on top of one another in an accordion fashion, so that he could carry them through.

"What time is Neil coming by the way?" he asked.

"Not sure, my guess is that he'll be here by the third of our video extravaganza!" Jo said, following them back to the couch; Laura carried four wine glasses and a bowl of popcorn.

"Let's get this show on the road then," Nick suggested.

They busied themselves laying their treats on the coffee table and then piled on to the couch. Nick enjoyed spending time with them. He knew they were going to have as much fun as they normally did, but he couldn't stop a part of him wishing he had Laura all to himself this weekend. Jo and Neil were staying until Laura's party on Sunday afternoon, because their house was being refurbished. They were evidently serious about moving back permanently, and were preparing their home to move in full time.

He looked down at Laura, and resigned himself to the fact that he would have to be patient. He didn't normally expect her all to himself, but they had not seen much of each other lately.

"I've missed nights like these," Jo sighed, with a mouth full of candy.

"Me too," Nick agreed.

"Me three," Laura laughed, raising her glass in the air. "Here's to old friends."

"To us" Nick and Jo said in unison, as they toasted one another.

They all settled down, instantly engrossed in the film; before the next one, they would pause to discuss it in great depth, as they had always done.

Nick switched on his radio to relieve the boredom of traveling in rush hour traffic. He had been to buy Laura a present for her birthday, but he hadn't planned on spending so much time deliberating the perfect gift. It was usually easy, so easy in fact that the awkwardness he felt in choosing something, took him by complete surprise.

Nick hated to sit in traffic; he usually took his bike to work and had been known to set off earlier than necessary to beat the rush. Still, he had what he ventured out for; he just hoped it was worth it.

He felt like a teenager sometimes, the excitement that took hold of him when he thought of her. It wasn't new to him, and he knew it would never fade. He had felt it since he first saw her in nursery all dressed in blue, though he hadn't known how to interpret it at the time.

Even though that were true, he had never know this kind of happiness. There had been times in his life when she made him feel like the only person in the world. It wasn't the big things she did; the little ones meant so much more. Like the time they were about seven or eight and Laura announced to the whole playground that Nick was her best friend in the world, or when she was sixteen and some idiot had rugby tackled her on the playing field. It had been Laura's party, so she was surrounded by family and friends. Nick could picture it now - everyone rushed forward in concern because she was hurt. She got up, and could have walked to anyone, but she chose Nick. She ran into his arms and held him so tightly he never wanted to let her go. He still felt that way.

A buzzing in Nick's ear made him jump in alarm; his head had been in a different place, which was not a good idea under normal driving conditions. Glancing at the dashboard, he noticed that Laura was calling; she always seemed to do that.

"I was just thinking about you," he spoke into his hands free receiver, after accepting the call.

"My ear was burning, or itching, or maybe it was my hand – one or the other!" Laura laughed softly in his ear.

"Did I ever tell you how much I like your laugh?" he wondered out loud.

"You haven't told me today yet!"

"Well now I have. How are you?" Nick asked, distracted for a second when a car cut in front of him.

"Very well, thanks. I'm just ringing to check if I will see you this evening?"

"I'm well too thanks!" he teased.

"Are you deliberately avoiding the question, or do you genuinely think I'm rude?" Laura joined in.

"Neither. I'm just trying to keep you on the phone longer!"

"Well, you will work such long shifts - it feels like weeks since we were alone," Laura said.

"You just want my body!"

"True," she agreed.

"That's weird, and I mean it in the nicest possible way!" Nick said, his voice deepening at the mere suggestion that she wanted him.

"It's that new aftershave, I can't control myself!"

"Touché," Nick laughed, enjoying their banter. "You are going to have to wait a little while longer though; I'm entertaining Jo and Neil again this evening."

"Ah yes, about that. I just spoke to Jo and explained how unfortunate it was that you had an emergency to attend to, which would probably keep you out all night," Laura informed him, sounding very pleased with herself.

"How very clever of you. In that case, I will be there in ten!" he answered, his heart accelerating in anticipation.

"I was hoping you'd say that."

"No, you knew I'd say that. How could I miss the opportunity to spend a whole evening with you, especially as you find me so irresistible?"

"Seriously though Nicky - you don't mind me reorganising your evening do you?"

"You know the answer to that, Blue," he said, not used to her insecurity.

"It's just all a bit new to us though isn't it?"

"Yes, in one way it is. But think about it from a purely friendship point of view. I love spending time with you, I always have, and it's not the first time you've made sure we got to see each other when my working hours were too crazy," Nick pointed out.

"I know, you're right. It's just that now…" Laura paused for a moment, as if struggling with the words. "Now, it's almost as though I can't get enough of you, holding you, touching you, kissing you…"

"Honey, I am trying to drive here!"

"Sorry," she laughed seductively, not sounding in the least bit remorseful.

"Go, woman, so I don't write my car off trying to reach you," Nick growled.

"What's taking you so long anyway?"

"As a matter of fact, I'm just pulling up outside."

"I'll meet you half way!" she laughed again.

"Damn good stuff this aftershave…" Nick started to say, but it was too late, she had gone.

Hurrying from the car, he walked towards the steps to Laura's apartment. She was already half way down them. He suddenly felt like the boy standing on that ruby field all those years ago, only this time, his thoughts were not as pure.

As they met at the bottom of the staircase - Laura at the same level due to the extra steps - she threw her arms around him and kissed him forcefully. Nick wrapped his own arms around her, and picked her up; he intended to eradicate any insecurity she had about orchestrating this particular meeting.

Chapter Twenty-three

Dear Matt

This is a hard entry for me to write, but I can't avoid it any longer. I wanted to be honest with you; I just didn't know what to say before. As usual, it takes me a while to get to the point.

I want to tell you about my new relationship with Nick. We have started to have romantic feelings for one another, and in the past year or so we have been particularly close. I know we've always had a strong friendship, but we have never relied on each other as much as we do now.

You've always been so understanding about Nicky, and I hope you understand this. I'm not telling you on a whim, I love him, and I want to make him happy.

It will never change what we had, or my love for you. I carry a piece of you around with me in my heart, and I will never let it go.

Until the next time my love,
Laura x

Laura smiled down at her words, relieved she had written them, but a little sad knowing they could hurt him. It was difficult loving two men at the same time. It was harder to accept the depth of her feelings for Nick, when she didn't think it was possible to love anyone else the way she had loved her husband. Laura did not, and would never compare them. Nick had always had the advantage because of their history.

She tried to explain to people how she felt about him, but it seemed too much for them to understand. Now that they were lovers, those same people were probably congratulating themselves for being right all along; she had wanted more than his friendship. It angered Laura, yet now she understood it.

She had always found Nick an attractive man, and accepted that women found him desirable, but she had genuinely become a better person because of their friendship. When she looked back, she realised that she had trivialised his good looks, because to think of him as a sexual being would have complicated a mutually beneficial relationship.

She now knew that her feelings for him had changed over the past twelve months without her realising it. She had looked forward to their weekly rendezvous more and more, and whenever she thought about him, it made her happy. It never occurred to her that these were romantic feelings, because he had always been the person who could raise her spirits.

Now, on the other hand, when she saw him, her pulse began to quicken. Where once she had looked into his kind face with the familiarity of a dear friend, she now couldn't look at him without wanting to kiss his mouth. It was all rather confusing when she analysed it too much, as she was doing now.

She replaced the journal in her desk drawer, and caught sight of her reflection in the dressing table mirror. Her hand automatically went to the pendant Nick bought her as a birthday gift. It was breathtaking in its simplicity; a fine platinum chain held a diamond in the shape of a heart, with an outline of sapphires. With a smile she went to get ready for her date with Nick. In the past couple of weeks they had both been busy, only snatching a few moments together here and there.

Laura had just signed a contract with Duncan Thomas, employing him as an in-house training provider, with a part share in the company. It felt good to be able to rely on someone else, and she couldn't' think of anyone she would rather share her vision with.

The team missed Charlie, but Laura was glad she moved to Scotland, because she knew the change was what she needed. She agreed to pay Charlie for the entire period of her temporary contract so that she didn't have to worry about the financial implications, whilst she found her feet.

This was Laura's first free night in the past week, and as Nick's schedule was also free, he had offered to cook for her. Digging through her wardrobe, she found the perfect dress; she had bought it for her sister's birthday, but it hadn't fit until now. Laura dressed quickly - she looked a little overdressed for a casual dinner for two, but it somehow felt right. She checked her hair one more time, enjoying the fluttering in her stomach, and went in search of her car keys.

Laura stood at Nick's door; her hand paused in mid air. She could hear him singing from within his apartment, and it made her smile. He usually sang when he was trying to release nervous energy. She had known him to get most of his work done with the volume turned up on his favourite song, joining in at the chorus. Finally connecting with the door, she wrapped her knuckles against the wood. Nick didn't keep her waiting long. It amused her even more than the singing when he quickly turned the music off.

As he swung the door open, he started to say something, but stopped when he took in her appearance. Laura saw his eyes darken, and giggled wickedly.

"Are you going to invite me in, or stand there gawping all evening?" she asked him.

"Hush," Nick answered, putting a finger to his lips, "I want to savour this moment."

Laura stepped forward and took his collar in both hands; knowing her intention, Nick allowed himself to be manipulated forward so she could kiss him. "Good evening," Laura whispered against his mouth.

"Good evening."

"What's for dinner, I'm starving?" she asked, stepping back.

Nick's eyes twinkled with mischief. "If you are hungry for food, you shouldn't have worn that dress!"

"Feed me, Carey, you know how grumpy I get when I'm not fed," she said with a laugh, pushing him aside so she could pass.

This time it was Laura's turn to be overwhelmed. There were candles everywhere, glittering like tiny fairy lights. Nick's moderate dining table had been transformed and now looked fit for a banquet. "Nicky, I'm speechless," Laura said, turning to him.

"I'm glad you like it. I want this evening to be special," he whispered, kissing the top of her head. "This way my lady!" he added dramatically, leading her to the table.

Nick had planned everything to perfection; her favourite wine, dishes she enjoyed, and soft music in the background. It was one of the best evenings Laura could remember in a while; she enjoyed their banter, playful flirting and most of all the laughter that came with an evening together. They took their time with their food, and chatted easily for hours. Laura felt totally at peace, especially since verbalising her feelings in her journal,

"Dance with me?" Nick said, as she was finishing the last mouthful of cheesecake.

"Anytime," she replied, standing to accept his invitation.

Nick wrapped his arms around her, and danced to the rhythm of the song; he was a strong lead, so she didn't have to think too much about it. Laying her head against Nick's chest, Laura signed in contentment. "There really is no better place than this."

"I couldn't agree with you more, which is why I organised tonight," Nick admitted, looking down at her as the song finished.

"That's a very serious tone, Mr. Carey." She felt a little nervous.

"I need to talk to you about something," he said, leading her to the couch.

"You're scaring me now."

"Laura, we've had a wonderful evening, and I'm not going to spoil things by rushing you and whipping a ring out of my pocket," he began, taking her hand. "I just need to tell you that at some point, soon I hope, I will be asking you that all important question."

"Nicky…" she began.

"No, don't interrupt. I want to say this." Laura nodded her head in consent.

"The fact of the matter, what I am trying to say, is that I want to spend the rest of my days being your best friend, your lover, and your confidant. I want to be a father to our children. I love you, Laura."

Laura took his face in her hands and kissed him gently; she had tears in her eyes. "Nicky, I love you too, with everything I have in my heart. I cannot see a future without you, nor do I want to. You know me so well, and I am thankful that you are giving me time, but the answer will be that I too, want to grow old loving you and only you."

Nick smiled at her words, leaning to kiss a stray tear on her cheek. "Thank you," he said softly, traveling down to her lips with soft kisses.

Laura responded against his mouth, her excitement growing, as it always did when he kissed her that way. "I'm hungry," she whispered, watching the colour deepen in his eyes.

"You're wearing the right dress. I like how easy it looks to take off!" With one swift movement she was in his arms. Laura laughed, laying her head against his shoulder, as he carried her to the bedroom.

About the Author

Melissa Barker-Simpson is a single mother, with two small children who keep her on her toes. They are the most challenging, yet rewarding part of her life, and she is constantly amazed by them.

She has a passion for language - although she writes as often as possible, her full time role is that of a British Sign Language/English Interpreter.

In her working life, she is the editor of a quarterly magazine run by her professional organisation, as well as the chair of a working group, administering a continual professional development programme.

Printed in the United Kingdom
by Lightning Source UK Ltd.
130596UK00002B/55/P